Santa Paws
and the New Puppy

Don't miss these other thrilling books in the
Santa Paws series:

SANTA PAWS

THE RETURN OF SANTA PAWS

SANTA PAWS, COME HOME

SANTA PAWS TO THE RESCUE

SANTA PAWS, OUR HERO

Santa Paws and the New Puppy

by Nicholas Edwards

AN
APPLE
PAPERBACK

SCHOLASTIC INC.

New York   Toronto   London   Auckland   Sydney
Mexico City   New Delhi   Hong Kong   Buenos Aires

No part of this publication may be reproduced in whole or in part, or stored in a retrieval system, or transmitted in any form or by any means, electronic, mechanical, photocopying, recording, or otherwise, without written permission of the publisher. For information regarding permission, write to Scholastic Inc., Attention: Permissions Department, 557 Broadway, New York, NY 10012.

ISBN 0-439-56075-6

Designed by Steve Scott

12 11 10 9 8   7 8/0

Printed in the U.S.A.

First Scholastic printing, November 2003

Santa Paws and the New Puppy

1

The dog opened his eyes, and yawned. What a wonderful nap he had just had! Better than usual, even. His family, the Callahans, had a big house, *full* of comfortable places to sleep. The dog had never been able to choose his favorite spot, so every day, he took turns trying out different places. There were couches and rugs and beds and chairs and fireplace hearths — and once, he had even sprawled out in an empty bathtub. But it felt too slippery and cold, so he had climbed out and curled up on the fluffy bath mat, instead.

There were nice places to relax out in the backyard, too. He didn't really like to lie in the snow, but grass, and dry leaves, and mud, and big piles of dirt were all fun. Flowerbeds were very cozy, too. When he walked around the town on a warm day, sometimes he liked to trot over to the beach and rest in the sand for a while. Unless he got too tired, and decided to take a little nap in the park, first. Sleeping in the Callahans' car was great, too. He especially liked the front seat.

Right now, he was up on Gregory's bed, with his head resting on the pillow. He felt a little bit thirsty, but it seemed too far to walk all the way downstairs to his water bowl. Maybe he would have more energy after another nap. That seemed like a good plan, so he yawned again and closed his eyes.

He was sound asleep when something heavy suddenly landed on top of him. The dog yelped in surprise, but then saw that it was just his cat friend, Abigail. He wagged his tail, and she swung her paw and whacked him across the muzzle in response. Then she sat on top of the pillow right next to his head, and started to wash her face.

The dog was still very tired, but he was nervous about closing his eyes with Abigail perched only a couple of inches away from him. He moved his head towards the other side of the pillow — which only gave Abigail an opportunity to sprawl across the entire thing. She was a very small cat, but somehow, she always managed to take up *a lot* of space. There was no room left for him at all, so he got up and moved down to the bottom of the bed. There was a thick afghan folded there, and it felt almost as soft as the pillow had.

It maybe wasn't a perfect place for a nap, but it was still very nice.

Once she had finished washing her face, Abigail stretched her paws out to admire her claws. She thought they were very pretty, indeed. And if she sharpened them later, on the kitchen table leg, they would be even *prettier*. Sometimes, one of the people in the house — usually Mrs. Callahan — would trim her nails with a terrible metal tool, and Abigail would have to growl and hiss and meow bitterly the entire time. The Callahans were very nice human beings, but she did not always approve of the way they behaved. Once, a couple of years earlier, when she had been coughing and sneezing, they had even given her pills from the vet! For several days in a row! It was awful, and she had been watching them carefully ever since to make sure that it didn't happen again.

At the bottom of the bed, the dog's legs moved restlessly, and he whimpered a few times as though he might be having a bad dream. Abigail thought it was very boring to watch him sleep. He was also much too noisy, in her opinion. Besides, the sun streaming in through the windows had started shining directly on the afghan, and it was her rightful duty to claim the spot for herself.

So she pounced on his stomach as hard as she

could to wake him up. The dog was startled and upset by this, which pleased her a great deal. He sat up, blinking in confusion, and she took his place on the afghan. The sun felt very soothing, and Abigail purred for a minute, before falling fast asleep.

The dog didn't want her to jump on him anymore, so he got off the bed. Maybe, if he went downstairs, Mr. Callahan would let him go outside for a while. Even better, he might get a Milk-Bone when he came back inside! His family *always* gave him a Milk-Bone after he had been out in the backyard, but he worried that they might forget someday, and then what would he do? It was too horrible to imagine.

He trotted downstairs to look for Mr. Callahan. The rest of the family, except for Abigail, and his other cat friend, Evelyn, wasn't home, which made him sad. Mrs. Callahan had been gone for a very long time — almost three days! — and he wondered when she would be coming back. He missed her very much. Gregory and Patricia had left right after eating breakfast that morning. It was terrible when they were away, and on most weekday afternoons, he would start waiting by the door for them right after lunch.

The dog loved his whole family, but Gregory and Patricia were his special favorites. A long time ago, he had been a lonely stray. He tried never to think about that bad time, but sometimes, when he was asleep, he would dream about it. He would be afraid when he woke up, until he saw that he was safe at his family's house, and that everything was okay.

One day, before he had a home of his own, he had met a friendly boy on the playground at an elementary school. It turned out to be Gregory, and the dog ended up getting to live with him and the rest of the Callahans. He was so lucky!

This year, Gregory was fifteen, and going to the high school for the first time. It was funny, because his voice was different now. He sounded almost like Mr. Callahan, and the dog thought that was strange. When he met Gregory, his voice had been much higher, and now it was deep! But it also sounded happy, especially when he came home from school and said things like, "Hey there, Big Guy, who's my best dog?" The dog would bark and jump on him, and sometimes they would even do a little dance together.

Patricia had just turned sixteen, and now she could drive! The dog was very surprised the first time he got into the car, and saw that she was behind the wheel. Because she only had her learner's permit, Mr. or Mrs. Callahan always sat in the passenger's seat next to her. Patricia was small for her age, and actually had to sit on a thick cushion, so that she could get a better view through the windshield — but she kept telling people that she only used the pillow to support her lumbar region.

Would they be home soon? The dog hoped so. On most days, they didn't return until it was dark out! That meant that he still had a very, very long time to wait.

The dog went straight to the den, but Mr. Callahan was not sitting at his desk. He was a writer, so during the day, he spent most of his time working at his computer. Or, at least, sitting at his desk and *looking* at the computer. And he wasn't lying on the couch, watching television, either.

The dog went back upstairs to check Mr. and Mrs. Callahan's bedroom, in case Mr. Callahan was taking a nap of his own. But, he wasn't there. Maybe he was admiring the Christmas tree? The dog ran down to the living room, and saw the tree, and the piles of presents, but no Mr. Callahan. Where could he be? Did he go somewhere, without even saying good-bye? This was terrible!

The dog decided to get a drink of water to make himself feel better — and found Mr. Callahan slouching at the kitchen table, with a mug of coffee. He was frowning, and staring down at a legal pad with lots of scribbling on it.

The dog woofed, very gently.

Mr. Callahan looked up from his legal pad. "Oh,

6

hi, Santa Paws," he said, his voice distracted. "Would you like to go out?"

The dog woofed more enthusiastically. Mr. Callahan was very smart, to guess what he wanted so quickly.

Although he answered to any name he heard, the dog's favorite was "Santa Paws." All of the people in town knew who he was, and they would wave and shout his name whenever they saw him. That made him happy, and he would bark and wag his tail at them. He liked it that everyone was always so nice to him.

The dog sat patiently next to the back door, but Mr. Callahan didn't come over. So, after a minute, he barked a very soft bark.

"Oh. Right." Mr. Callahan shook his head, and then got up to open the door. "Have fun, buddy."

Yes! "Buddy" was a good name, too! The dog galloped out into the backyard. There was snow on the ground, which had started to melt and then, froze again overnight. That left an icy crust on top of the drifts, and the dog's feet kept breaking through and getting caught. But, he still liked it!

He was pretty sure he saw a seagull gliding over the yard, so he barked wildly. It might just have been a piece of paper blowing in the wind — but, it was still worth a few minutes of barking. If he saw a squirrel, that would be *great*. He lifted his nose to sniff the air, but mostly, he could only smell the ocean. And, someplace nearby, he could smell meat. Pot roast!

The dog turned towards the back door, wondering if Mr. Callahan had started cooking supper already. No, the smell was coming from their neighbors' house. He ran down to the corner of the yard and lifted his paws up on top of the fence. Were *they* making supper? He sniffed some more, until he decided that the delicious smell was coming from the Robinsons' trash cans.

They put *pot roast* in the *trash*? The dog tensed his hind legs, trying to decide whether he should hop over the fence. It would be very, very wrong to tip over the trash can. He might even get told "No!" or "Bad dog!" Those words always hurt his feelings, along with "Stay!" and "Lie down!" Being told that he was bad was the very worst, though.

What if he didn't tip it all the way over, and just poked his head inside? Would that be okay? The dog liked to be good — even when he was very hungry. But maybe if he just walked by the trash cans, right next to them, they would fall over, and then it would be okay to have a snack.

If Abigail came outside, she would probably knock the can down *for* him. She liked to be bad. She was supposed to stay in the house, though, and only snuck out when she thought he might be going someplace fun without her. Evelyn *never* came outside, unless she was in her carrier, where she felt safe.

A car horn beeped, and the dog turned towards the street. It had come from a minivan full of Cub Scouts, all of whom waved enthusiastically and yelled, "Hi, Santa Paws!" as the car drove by. The dog wagged his tail and ran over to watch them go. He wasn't exactly sure who they were, but they were still his friends!

Once the minivan turned the corner, the dog ran around the yard in circles. It had just started snowing again, and he liked to try and race between the flakes, if he could. But then, suddenly, he stopped short.

Somewhere, something was wrong. Someone was in trouble. He closed his eyes and lifted one paw, so he could concentrate. He was very good at sensing when there was danger, but sometimes it took him a minute or two to *locate* it. Once he was sure he knew the right direction, the dog dashed towards the gate and sailed gracefully right over it.

He ran steadily in the direction of the Oceanport Nature Appreciation Society building. It was several blocks away, and located on a dead-end road by the woods. There was a hilly meadow right next to the parking lot, and during the winter, people in the town often went sledding there. Today, three eighth-graders were taking turns careening down the slope on an old wooden sled.

Unfortunately, one of them — a girl named Mary-Beth — had just skidded out of control and crashed right into a tree! Now her ankle was so swollen and painful that she was afraid she might have broken it.

"Maybe we should carry her to the hospital," her twin brother, Eric, said uncertainly.

Their friend Natisha looked doubtful. "I think we might hurt her worse that way." She checked her pockets. "I forgot my cell phone — do you have one?"

Eric found his inside his jacket, but when he looked at the display, he could see that the battery was dead. "I left it on too long again," he said. "Maybe we should just go for help?"

Mary-Beth looked alarmed. "And *leave* me here? What if forest monsters show up?" She was a fairly jittery person, and had always believed in goblins, and leprechauns, and unicorns — and just about every single mysterious thing she had *ever* seen on television.

Eric and Natisha considered that possibility.

"Does Oceanport have forest monsters?" Eric asked. Unlike his twin, he didn't believe in much of anything unusual, unless there were eyewitnesses, photographic evidence, and maybe even some DNA to prove it.

Natisha had no opinion about magical beings whatsoever, so she just shrugged. "Does *any-place* have forest monsters?"

10

They both thought some more.

"England," Eric said, very confident. "They all think they have that Loch Ness monster-thing."

"That isn't really a forest monster," Natisha pointed out. "It's more like a water-monster."

"It's also in *Scotland*, not England," Mary-Beth said, through pain-gritted teeth. She was trying not to cry, but she couldn't help it, because her ankle hurt so much. "Look, it's going to be dark soon. One of you guys has to go find some help."

Eric nodded. "Good plan."

"Absolutely," Natisha agreed.

So Eric jogged off towards their house, half a mile away. Their parents probably weren't home from work yet, but he could call "911" from there.

It was snowing harder now, and the daylight was definitely turning into dusk. Natisha helped Mary-Beth back up onto the sled, so at least she wouldn't be sitting in the cold snow while they waited.

Just then, they saw a large furry shape tearing across the meadow towards them.

"Whoa," Natisha said. "Forest monster!"

Mary-Beth's eyes widened. Then she realized that her friend was kidding her, and she relaxed.

It was Santa Paws, coming to the rescue!

2

Santa Paws was very upset to see an injured girl in the snow. He knew he needed to help her, but he wasn't sure how. Should he go to the building where the nice men and women in the uniforms worked? Then he could get them to drive their cars and trucks with the lights and sirens over here to pick the girl up. It would take him a long time to run down there, though, and it was getting dark.

Mary-Beth and Natisha looked at each other. Naturally, they had read all about the famous hero, Santa Paws, over the years. They had each even seen him in person a couple of times, being walked by his owners, or running through the streets of Oceanport on his way to solve a problem somewhere. Many nights, his exploits were the top story on the television news, and last month, he had been on the cover of a regional magazine. But they had never been rescued by him before and weren't sure exactly how it worked.

"Hi, Santa Paws," Natisha said tentatively.

The dog wagged his tail, and lifted his paw for her to shake. Then he shook paws with Mary-Beth, too.

"He's not really a purebred German shepherd, is he," Mary-Beth said, looking him over critically, although she enjoyed shaking his paw. "They're always saying he's a German shepherd on the news, but I don't think so. He's a mongrel."

"Part collie, maybe?" Natisha guessed.

"That sounds right," Mary-Beth said. "Although the media should really *report* that, I think. Instead of getting it wrong."

The dog was still trying to make up his mind about what to do. Was there a kind neighbor living nearby? Should he go to a street with lots of passing traffic and bark until someone stopped to see what was wrong?

Natisha looked very disappointed. "I was hoping that he could talk. I was reading on the Internet that Santa Paws speaks perfect English when there aren't any adults around."

"Maybe his cut-off point is — I don't know — ten years old," Mary-Beth said. "We might be over the age limit."

Then, Santa Paws saw the rope looped around

the front of the sled. He knew just what to do! He dropped down into the snow and wriggled underneath the rope. Then he stood up, with the rope between his teeth. He took a deep breath and started pulling the sled across the meadow.

Mary-Beth was so surprised that she immediately fell off, and Santa Paws stopped in his tracks. Natisha helped her get climb back on, and the dog began pulling again. Luckily, she wasn't very heavy, and there was enough fresh snow on the ground to make the sled easy to move.

"Where do you think we're going?" Mary-Beth asked, as he took them up one street, and down another.

"I don't know," Natisha said, since they were heading in the opposite direction of their homes. "Maybe he's lost." She had always assumed that Santa Paws, like Santa *Claus*, knew exactly where everyone lived, without having to be told.

The dog carefully turned down a third street, making sure to keep the sled sliding smoothly so that Mary-Beth wouldn't tumble off again. Just up ahead was the office where his friend Dr. Kasanofsky worked. Whenever the dog got hurt or didn't feel good, the Callahans would bring him here for a check-up, and he *always* felt better after that. He dragged the sled right up to the front door and then barked loudly.

After a moment, the door opened and one of the veterinary assistants looked out.

"Dr. K.!" she called. "Santa Paws is here to visit!"

Dr. Kasanofsky came out right away, wearing his white lab coat. The office had been getting ready to close, but he was always happy to see Santa Paws, no matter what time it was. He also knew Natisha, whose family brought their cats to him.

"Well, hi," he said. "Did you all just stop by to say hello? Are you giving free rides today, Santa Paws?"

Natisha looked perplexed. "You're a vet, Dr. K."

"Yes," Dr. Kasanofsky agreed, somewhat puzzled by that. "I'm a vet."

"Can you fix my ankle?" Mary-Beth asked. "Or do I need a pediatrician?"

Once Dr. Kasanofsky realized what was actually going on, he quickly sent his assistant inside to call for an ambulance to take Mary-Beth to the Emergency Room, and to put a call through to her parents, too. In the meantime, he brought her inside his office to elevate her leg and put an ice pack on it. He also patted Santa Paws and gave him two biscuits.

"Thank you, Santa Paws," he told him. "You are a very good dog."

The dog wagged his tail. "Good dog" was one of his favorite things to hear! Once he had finished eating his biscuits — they were delicious! — he headed for the door and used his paw to push it open. It was going to be suppertime soon, and he really wanted to get home.

"Wait," Dr. K. called after him. "We'll get someone to come pick you up!"

But, the dog was already gone.

By the time the dog made it back to his house, it was dark out. He jumped over the gate and ran straight to the door. When Mrs. Callahan came to let him in, he was filled with joy. She was home! She had been gone for *so* long, but now she was here! And maybe Gregory and Patricia were home, too.

"Hi, Santa Paws," she said, and patted him.

The dog barked happily as she took down the Milk-Bones box from the top of the refrigerator.

"I'm not sure I want to know where exactly you've been," she said wryly, and then gave him a biscuit. "I'm glad you're back, though."

The dog wagged his tail and settled down on his special red rug to enjoy his Milk-Bone. Evelyn, the elderly tiger cat, came wandering into the kitchen, and the dog hunched protectively over his biscuit. But Evelyn just sniffed disdainfully in his general direction, and jumped up onto the kitchen table. She knocked over a large stack of mail and magazines in the process, but Mrs. Callahan just patted her and picked them up.

"I think it's time to feed everyone, don't you?" she said.

16

Feed? The dog knew *that* word! Yay!

In the upstairs bathroom, Abigail was busy trying to climb the shower curtain when she heard the distinctive click of the can opener. She tore downstairs, leaped onto the kitchen table — and knocked all of the mail and magazines right back onto the floor, as well as a wooden bowl full of fruit and two candlesticks.

"Very graceful, Abigail," Mrs. Callahan said.

Abigail purred in a very charming way, switching her tail back and forth — which tipped over a flower vase.

Mrs. Callahan watched as daisies and water spilled all over the linoleum. "Nice job," she said. "That was a clean sweep, Abigail."

Abigail purred even harder.

As Mrs. Callahan was serving each of the animals some canned supper, the door banged open. Patricia and Gregory came into the house, loaded down with backpacks, sports equipment, snow-covered jackets, and — in Patricia's case — a very large double-latte.

"Hey, Mom!" Gregory said cheerfully. He took off his Red Sox cap and shook some of the snow off it. "When'd you get home?" He paused to pat Santa Paws, who wagged his tail, but kept eating.

"Just about an hour ago," Mrs. Callahan said. "My plane was running late because of the weather."

"What happened?" Patricia asked, looking at the mess on the floor. "Have a little tantrum?"

"Big tantrum," Mrs. Callahan said briefly.

Patricia grinned and dumped her hockey gear in the corner. "Sorry I missed it." She dropped her knapsack onto the table and bent to start picking up the water-soaked mail and magazines.

"Who drove you home?" Mrs. Callahan asked, as she ripped off some paper towels to wipe away the spilled water — and the snow Gregory and Patricia had just tracked inside.

"Oscar's mother," Gregory said. Oscar was his best friend, and they were both first-year players on the high school basketball team. They liked basketball pretty well, but they *loved* football. Even now, weeks after the season was over, they still spent a lot of time in the school weight room, working out with other members of the team. Gregory had expected to be on the junior varsity, but to his delight, he had ended up on the varsity, playing both tight-end and cornerback.

"Because, you know, *some* parents enjoy coming to watch their children's sporting events," Patricia said sadly. Actually, one or both of her parents almost always came, but that was no reason not to make a joke about it. Except that she saw her mother's worried expression, and decided that this maybe wasn't an ideal time for goofing around. "Is Aunt Laurel feeling better?"

18

Aunt Laurel was actually their *great*-aunt, and she had been having some very serious health problems lately. As a result, Mrs. Callahan had had to make several unexpected trips to New York City, to visit and help take care of her during the past few months. There was even a possibility that the whole family might end up going down to spend the summer in the city, once school was out, so that Mrs. Callahan wouldn't have to keep traveling back and forth all the time. Aunt Laurel was one of Mrs. Callahan's only living relatives, and the two of them had always been extremely close.

"Unfortunately, no," Mrs. Callahan said. "In fact — " She stopped. "Why don't you two get cleaned up, and have a snack, and then come into the den, okay? Your father and I need to talk to you."

Gregory and Patricia looked at each other.

"Are we in trouble?" Gregory asked uneasily. He couldn't *think* of anything terrible they'd done lately, but maybe he was overlooking something.

Mrs. Callahan shook her head. "No, nothing like that. We just need to talk things over as a family."

Neither Gregory nor Patricia particularly liked the sound of that, but they nodded cooperatively and went upstairs to get cleaned up and change into fresh clothes. Gregory was still wearing his basketball uniform and warm-ups, while Patricia had a hockey jersey on over her jeans. She had gone straight from practice to watch the end of his game.

"Will you get upset if I say it's your fault?" Gregory asked as they headed back downstairs.

Patricia paused on the steps to look at him. "That what was my fault?"

Gregory shrugged. "I don't know. Whatever they're mad about."

"She said we weren't in trouble," Patricia reminded him.

"Well, yeah, but the last time we had a family meeting — " Gregory broke off his sentence. "Wait, have we *ever* had a family meeting?"

"Can't think of one, no," Patricia said. "Except maybe that time we were trying to decide whether to go to Disney World or Colonial Williamsburg."

Gregory nodded, remembering a long-ago breakfast conversation. And, in fact, in the end, they had decided to take a vacation to Chicago and, among other things, go to a day game at Wrigley Field. It had been an *excellent* trip.

"She just got back from New York," Patricia said logically. "So it's probably going to be about Aunt Laurel."

Gregory frowned. "I hope she's okay. I mean, she seems like the *last* person who would ever have anything wrong with her, you know?"

Patricia nodded. They were both very fond of Aunt Laurel. She had always been full of energy and fun, and loved nothing more than going out and trying to find adventures. But recently, she had become increasingly disabled by rheumatoid arthritis and there was a chance that she might be forced to use a wheelchair permanently. The thought of that was so upsetting that none of them really wanted to think about it. It seemed better to talk about *when* she would get well, not *if* she would get well.

They walked into the den to find their father leaning against his desk, with his arms folded, and their mother sitting on the love seat, while Evelyn slept on her lap.

"So," Gregory said uneasily, and put his hands in his pockets.

"Is this the kind of conversation where I'm going to have to make a quick exit, run upstairs, and slam my door really hard?" Patricia asked.

Both of her parents winced.

"Boy, I hope not," Mr. Callahan said. "That would be awfully loud."

Since Patricia was more of a confrontational make-as-many-snide-remarks-as-possible type, it was probably a moot point, anyway.

It was quiet for a minute, and they all looked at one another, waiting for someone else to start.

"Well," Mrs. Callahan said. "I — "

Having just finished his supper — as well as

half of Evelyn's and a stray potato chip he found on the floor — the dog bounced into the room and took turns greeting each of them with great affection. It broke the tension, and everyone relaxed a little.

"Should we light a fire and roast some chestnuts?" Patricia asked. "Really hammer in this family togetherness thing?"

"Sure," Mrs. Callahan said. "We'll send Santa Paws out to the yard to gather some."

Hearing his name, the dog thumped his tail on the floor. But he didn't bother getting up, because he was busy chewing on an old tennis ball he had just found under the rocking chair.

Mr. Callahan cleared his throat. "Your mother and I need to talk to you about Aunt Laurel's situation. She's having a really hard time, and we're trying to figure out the best way to help her."

"Is she going back in the hospital?" Gregory asked.

"Well, for a second hip replacement, for sure," Mrs. Callahan said. "But, with the rheumatoid arthritis getting worse, she's also going to need some long-term — " She sighed. "The children make it much more complicated."

Aunt Laurel had never been able to have children, so for years, she had taken in a series of foster children. Their Great-Uncle Mortimer had died when Gregory was little, but Aunt Laurel had continued to be a foster parent. Right now, two children named Pedro and Kate lived with her. Pedro was almost eleven, and Kate had just turned nine. Aunt Laurel had been in perfect health for years, and was actually in the process of formally adopting them. The adoptions were almost final, and Mr. and Mrs. Callahan were going to be their godparents. And Patricia and Gregory were pretty happy about the idea of Pedro and Kate *officially* becoming their cousins.

"So, maybe they should all come up here to stay for a while," Patricia suggested.

"Well, we thought of that," Mrs. Callahan said, "but Aunt Laurel really *loves* New York. It's her home. And she's worked so hard to make Pedro and Kate feel safe and secure, that we wouldn't want to do anything to upset that. We'd really like to find a way to help them be able to stay there. And we don't want to take any chance of the adoptions not going through, so we have to consider that, too."

Patricia had a sinking feeling that she knew where this conversation was going, but Gregory was still trying to figure it out.

"So, like, wait," he said. "You don't mean you want *us* to move to New York, do you?"

His parents nodded.

"Yes," Mrs. Callahan said. "That's exactly what we want."

3

If it had been quiet in the room a few minutes earlier, now it was absolutely *silent*. Gregory and Patricia stared at their parents.

"Move to New York City?" Gregory asked, again.

"As opposed to what," Patricia said sarcastically, "New York *Country*?"

The dog stopped chewing his tennis ball. Were Gregory and Patricia angry? It sounded that way, and he didn't like it when they got upset.

Gregory scowled at her. "I'm just asking, okay? It's, like, totally weird, and — "

Patricia scowled back at him. "Yeah, well, I'm just asking *you* not to — "

Since it was pretty obvious that they were about to have a big argument, Mr. Callahan put his fingers in his mouth and whistled sharply. "That's the end of the round, guys. Go to separate corners."

At first, Gregory thought that he really did

24

want them to go stand in the corner, but then he caught on to the boxing metaphor and smiled a little. He punched Patricia lightly in the shoulder, and she gave him a slightly harder, but still friendly, punch back.

Everyone seemed happier now, and the dog went back to his tennis ball.

"Nothing's been decided," Mr. Callahan said calmly, now that peace had been restored. "Obviously, this would be a huge change for all of us, and naturally, that's why we wanted to discuss it with you. Anyway, we're not talking about a permanent move — it's more a question of our going down there temporarily, to help them through this rough patch. Sort of — a prolonged visit."

"We already talked about maybe being there this summer," Patricia pointed out. "Is that what you mean?"

Mrs. Callahan looked unhappy. "I don't think we can wait that long, Patricia. They *really* need our help now."

"I thought, in New York, that everyone had full-time maids and nannies, and stuff," Gregory said. He had read stories about it in magazines, and it seemed to be that way for characters on television and in the movies, too. "Like, living there, taking care of everything."

"Some New Yorkers do live that way," Mrs. Callahan conceded. "And, of course, Aunt Laurel has Thelma coming in, to help with the kids after school." They all really liked Thelma, who was very jolly and referred to herself as a "female majordomo," but mainly, she just did a little bit of babysitting. "Besides, Aunt Laurel's done so much for me, my whole life, and she's the only family I have left, and — " She let out her breath. "I really want to help her myself, but it's not very practical for me to be flying back and forth all the time. The school has been very nice about it so far, but they need to be able to make plans, too."

Mrs. Callahan taught physics at Oceanport High School, and she had been taking a lot of time off lately, while she traveled to New York. Then, whenever she came home, she would have to stay up, night after night, to catch up on all of the work she had missed. So she was always very tired, and Gregory and Patricia and their father had been worried about her.

"If we decided to do it, when would we go?" Patricia asked.

Mr. and Mrs. Callahan exchanged glances.

"Well, as soon as possible," Mr. Callahan said. "I've been making a lot of calls, and Columbia University is willing to let me be a Writer-in-Residence if I can get there in time for the new semester. So, that would be next month."

Patricia blinked, not sure if she had heard that correctly. "Next *month*?"

Their parents nodded.

Although Gregory and Patricia never thought of him that way, Mr. Callahan was actually a pretty famous writer, so it made sense that a university would want to hire him. His books were everywhere — even airport gift shops! — and sometimes he won prizes, too. But since he was so absent-minded that he regularly did things like go out in public in his slippers, they had a hard time picturing him as a hot-shot celebrity author.

Gregory had been slouching on the couch next to Patricia, but now, he sat up straight. "Hey, whoa. You mean, you'd have a *job*, Dad?"

"I already have a job," Mr. Callahan said defensively, and gestured towards his computer and the jumbled stack of pages from his latest manuscript.

"I meant a job where you go *outside*," Gregory said.

Mr. Callahan shrugged. "Well, as your mother pointed out, we'd all be facing some big changes in our lives."

Patricia and Gregory avoided each other's eyes, trying not to laugh. The image of their father in front of a classroom in one of his typical working outfits — complete with a goofy hat, ancient T-shirt, sweatpants, and fluffy bunny slippers — was pretty funny.

Mrs. Callahan stood up. "We don't have to make any final decisions right this moment. Why don't we all just think about it, for now, and in the meantime, let's go out to the kitchen and get some supper."

The dog's ears shot up. Supper? Was he getting a second supper? Oh, that would be *so fun*.

"Can we get pizza?" Gregory asked, just as Patricia was saying, "Chinese food."

"Or Mexican," Mr. Callahan said. "Mexican would be nice."

In the end, they ordered from a local Thai restaurant, instead. Without making a big issue of it, they kept the dinner table conversation restricted to normal subjects like school, and Gregory's basketball game, and what to do about the ever-increasing stack of fan mail for Santa Paws. They always tried to answer the letters as fast as possible, but it was easy to fall behind, especially around the holidays.

"Did he have any good rescues while I was gone?" Mrs. Callahan asked, as she finished her *Gai Tom Kha*, which was chicken and coconut milk soup.

Patricia shook her head. "Not really. Lost kittens, dragging children out of traffic, herding people from a burning house — the usual."

Mrs. Callahan nodded, since, for Santa Paws, that *was* business as usual.

"But, it was pretty cool when he helped those nuns get their boat off the sandbar," Gregory said.

"That was a good one," Mr. Callahan agreed, spooning a second helping of beef *satay* onto his plate.

"Sounds great. I'm sorry I missed it," Mrs. Callahan said, as she lifted Abigail away from the container of *pad thai*.

Terribly annoyed not to have been able to steal a shrimp or two for herself, Abigail flounced off to the living room. She planned to express her displeasure by eating several icicles from the Christmas tree, and vomiting them onto the first pillow she could find.

There was a stack of newspapers in the corner of the kitchen, waiting to be recycled, and Patricia went over to flip through the top of the pile. She retrieved the front page from two days earlier and handed it to her mother.

"Oh, my," Mrs. Callahan said. She had been expecting to see some nuns and a tiny dinghy, perhaps, but the large photo displayed a magnificent racing sloop, instead. And some nuns. To say nothing of Santa Paws tugging on a rope, to try and pull the boat upright. "What wonderful visuals."

Patricia nodded. "It was all over the news. We didn't even know what had happened, until we turned on the television."

"It *did* seem peculiar," Mr. Callahan said thoughtfully, "when he came home wearing a set of rosary beads."

After dinner, Gregory took Santa Paws for a completely uneventful walk in the snow. The dog loved to wrestle with Gregory, and they spent some time scuffling around in the backyard before coming inside. They found Patricia sitting at the kitchen table, doing her chemistry homework.

"Was I gone long enough for the dishes to be done?" Gregory asked.

"Yep," Patricia said. "Did you plan it that way?"

Gregory nodded.

"I figured," Patricia said, flipping to the next page in her textbook. "That's why I decided to let you set the table for breakfast."

Since that seemed like a fair trade, Gregory nodded agreeably. After drying Santa Paws off with a towel and taking off his own snowy boots, Gregory decided that it was time for a snack. He handed Santa Paws a Milk-Bone and fixed himself a huge bowl of mint chocolate chip ice cream with chocolate syrup, along with six butterscotch brownies. He thought about getting some corn chips, and maybe a couple of bananas, too, but decided to save that for a bedtime snack.

"You're a pig," Patricia said.

"Want me to burp really loud, too?" Gregory offered. On the football team, they sometimes had burping contests, and he had actually won two of them so far.

"Sounds fun," Patricia said, "but I'll pass, thanks."

Gregory checked to make sure that their parents were nowhere nearby and then, lowered his voice. "How upset are we?" he asked.

Patricia stopped writing immediately. "Pretty upset."

Gregory nodded. He knew he wasn't too happy about the idea of suddenly having to drop everything and move, but it was always nice to get a second opinion. "Just making sure. In case you were, you know, totally into the idea."

"I am completely *not* into the idea," Patricia said.

Gregory was a little bit relieved that they felt exactly the same way. If everyone else in the family was overjoyed about the idea of moving to New York, and he wasn't, he would feel like a jerk. "But, I guess we'll probably be good sports about it?"

Patricia sighed. "Yeah," she said. "We called Aunt Laurel while you were outside, and she was saying no, no, please don't come, I can take care of things — but I could tell she felt like crying. She sounded really tired, too."

Gregory nodded. Aunt Laurel wasn't the sort of person who had ever needed help, and he knew she must hate the idea of not being able to do everything for herself right now. "So, then, we'll definitely be good sports."

Patricia grinned a little. "We'll be *excellent* sports," she said.

The next morning, Mr. Callahan must have gotten up very early, because by the time everyone else came downstairs, he was in the middle of preparing a huge, homemade breakfast. He had even hiked several blocks through the snow to Leo's Bakery when it opened at six o'clock sharp to buy several loaves of bread, hot from the oven. Now he was cutting the bread into extra-thick slices, and using it to make cinnamon-flavored French toast. He had also cooked bacon and a large batch of fresh applesauce, from which he had managed to strain almost all of the seeds.

They all complimented him lavishly about his cooking, but other than that, the breakfast conversation was a little stilted. Finally, Patricia brought up the subject they had all been cautiously avoiding so far.

"So," she said, "how are we all going to fit in Aunt Laurel's apartment? I mean, maybe I could share Kate's room, and Gregory could go in with Pedro, but where would you and Dad sleep?"

Aunt Laurel had an old three-bedroom apartment on West End Avenue near 106ᵗʰ Street, which she and Uncle Mortimer had bought back many years ago, before real estate had become so expensive. By New York City standards, it was a very large living space, but it would be a tight fit for seven people, plus the cats and Santa Paws.

"She has some friends on the 8th floor who want to retire to Florida," Mrs. Callahan said. "For the time being, we could sublet from them, and see how things work out."

Gregory frowned. He wasn't completely sure what "sublet" meant, but he assumed that it was something like renting an apartment. "So then, we'd keep our house here?"

"Of course!" Mr. Callahan assured him. "This isn't a permanent move, remember? We're really thinking about something like six months. Or maybe we'll just stay down there until the end of the school year, and then we can all come back up here for the summer. I don't know — we'll have to play it by ear."

Gregory and Patricia were relieved to hear that. The idea of permanently leaving Oceanport, and their friends, and — well, their entire *lives* — was pretty overwhelming, but the thought of a more temporary stay wasn't nearly as intimidating.

"What about school?" Patricia asked.

Aunt Laurel had spent twenty-six years teaching history in the New York City public school system, and Gregory had an alarming thought. "Hey, yeah! We wouldn't have to be home-schooled or something, would we?"

Mrs. Callahan smiled at him. "No, don't worry. We'll make sure to find a good school for you two. Or, you might even want to go to different schools. There are lots of different options in a city that big."

Gregory wasn't too excited about the idea of having to go to an unfamiliar city school and be the "new kid," but now he had another worry. "My new school will have a football team, right?" he asked.

"We'll make sure of it," Mr. Callahan promised. "And we should be back here before next season starts, anyway. You'll just miss the spring practices."

"Maybe it shouldn't be a very *good* football team," Gregory said, after thinking about it for a minute. In a huge school, there were bound to be some really talented players. "So I, you know, have a decent chance of making it."

Mr. Callahan nodded, and pretended to write that down on his place mat. "A team with a losing record. Check." He turned to Patricia, already anticipating what she was about to say. "No, not too many schools down there have girls' hockey teams, but if we can't find one, I promise we'll get you into one of the amateur leagues they run down at Chelsea Piers, or someplace like that."

With her question answered before she had

even had a chance to ask it, Patricia just nodded and put more maple syrup on her French toast.

"What about you, Mom?" Gregory asked.

Mrs. Callahan shrugged. "I'll take a leave of absence from the high school. They'll probably just mark it down as a sabbatical."

There were many more questions to ask, but so far, it seemed as though Mr. and Mrs. Callahan already had most of the answers ready.

"So, it's okay with the two of you if your father and I start making some serious plans?" Mrs. Callahan asked.

Gregory and Patricia looked at each other, and then nodded.

They were moving to New York City!

4

The news that the Callahans — and more importantly, Santa Paws — were leaving Oceanport spread through the entire town with astonishing speed. Some people were just sad to hear the news, while others were downright alarmed about the prospect of not having Santa Paws nearby, watching over them at all times. One group of concerned citizens even marched down to the police station, to ask Chief Merloni how she was going to change her patrol deployment plans to make up for the increased protection the town would need. And Patricia's hockey coach was just plain crushed to be losing his star left-wing.

Santa Paws, of course, simply continued on with his normal everyday life, and his usual series of rescues. He did notice that there were suddenly lots of cardboard boxes all over the house, but he assumed that the Callahans *knew* that the boxes were there, and had a very good reason for keeping them around. Abigail and Evelyn thought the boxes were the best cat presents they had ever seen, and spent all of their time jumping in and out of them. As far as they were concerned, boxes were perfect for both hiding and sleeping, which were their very favorite things to do.

On Saturday afternoon, the week before Christmas, Gregory went outside to throw sticks for Santa Paws. He had been busy packing and sorting his stuff all day, and it was definitely time to get some fresh air. The temperature was much warmer than usual, and the snow was starting to melt. The weather channel had forecast heavy rain for the next couple of days, but so far, the sky seemed bright and clear.

Santa Paws would fetch for hours on end, if he could get someone to throw things for him, and his tail never stopped wagging as Gregory tossed sticks, an old baseball, and even a soggy mitten he found in a pile of snow.

Patricia came outside a little while later, all bundled up in her leather jacket, gloves, and a New England Patriots cap. Then she looked surprised.

"Hey, it's like fifty degrees out here," she said, unzipping the jacket. It was a vintage police motorcycle jacket their Uncle Steve had given her for her birthday. Uncle Steve was Mr. Callahan's little brother — and also, a Lieutenant on the

Oceanport Police Department. Since becoming a police officer was among Patricia's career goals — along with being a United States Supreme Court Justice, a Nobel Peace Prize winner, and possibly, a vampire slayer — she had really appreciated the gift. It was also a really cool-looking jacket, and she liked the fashion statement it made.

Santa Paws had just returned the battered baseball for the tenth consecutive time, and dropped it at Gregory's feet.

Gregory picked it up and threw it across the yard for him. He had discarded his ski jacket five minutes after coming outside because he got so hot, and it was now hanging from a nearby tree branch. "I know, it's really nice out. But I don't think it's going to be so great for the Ice Sculpture contest."

Every year, the town of Oceanport sponsored the "Festival of Many Lands" in the park. Oceanport was extremely multicultural, and enjoyed celebrating the customs of lots of different cultures during the holidays. There were always dozens of exhibits and booths set up in the park, along with a series of contests, games, and musical performances. The 37th Annual Ice Sculpture contest was scheduled for that night, but the warm weather was going to make that difficult. One year, the contest had been postponed until a cold snap hit a few days later, and this had been terribly disappointing for everyone involved. People in Oceanport took their local traditions very seriously.

As Gregory threw the baseball yet again, he noticed a boy running up the street as fast as he could. He stopped in front of their gate and waved his arms wildly.

"Help me!" he shouted, barely able to catch his breath. "Timmy fell down the well!"

Gregory laughed, while Patricia just rolled her eyes. Every now and then, they got prank phone calls, where someone shouted something like that into the telephone. Anything Lassie had ever done on television or in the movies, they liked to pretend that Santa Paws should do, too. Actually, Pedro — who was very mischievous — had been known to call them up and say just that sort of thing. It was unusual, though, to have someone actually show up at their house to play the trick in person.

The dog had recognized the word "Help!", but he wasn't sure why Gregory and Patricia were just standing there, looking bored. So he waited, instinctively lifting one paw. If there was trouble, he wanted to be ready to respond right away.

"We've heard that one before," Gregory said to the boy. "But, it's still pretty funny."

The boy looked stunned. "You aren't going to help me? I need help! Timmy's in the well!"

Hearing that word again — twice! — the dog whined a little.

"We have a television, too," Patricia said, not unkindly. "So we've seen the show, okay?"

By now, the boy was close to tears. "You don't understand. *Timmy fell in the well.*"

Gregory was starting to wonder if this kid had lost his mind when he realized that Santa Paws was standing in that unmistakably alert and anxious way he had seen so many times before. "Are you saying you actually know someone named Timmy?" he asked.

The boy rubbed his fist across his eyes, trying not to cry. "Yes. He's my little brother. Why won't Santa Paws help me?"

Since Gregory and Patricia didn't seem to know what to do, Santa Paws took the initiative and jumped over the fence. He turned his head in each direction, sniffing, and then ran up the street.

"An actual Timmy, in an actual well." Gregory paused. "Okay. I guess we're going to need some rope."

While Gregory and the boy grabbed some rope from the garage and headed after Santa Paws, Patricia took the time to go inside and call "911," first. The dispatcher who answered the call was both annoyed and amused by the nature of the complaint, and she had a hard time convincing him that she was telling the truth.

"No, this is a *real* person named Timmy, in a

real well," she was saying, as Mr. Callahan came into the kitchen to get some coffee. She listened for a minute. "No, I don't know exactly where the well is, I just, um — I know it's real."

Mr. Callahan normally didn't eavesdrop, but this conversation was too intriguing to pass up. He sat down at the table to listen, as she kept trying to persuade the dispatcher. Finally, she hung up in frustration and saw her father's curious expression.

"I, um, I guess you heard most of that," she said.

Mr. Callahan nodded solemnly. "Timmy fell in the well."

"Yeah. Santa Paws went to save him." Patricia stopped, aware of how silly this all sounded. "And — Gregory got some rope."

Mr. Callahan shrugged, quite willing to believe that. After all, it wasn't any more unusual than their dog's other heroic escapades. "Okay. Want to go find them? See if we can help?"

Patricia nodded, but pointed at his feet as he started to open the door.

Mr. Callahan looked down at his green dragon — complete with flames made of orange felt — slippers. "Right," he said, and went to get his winter boots.

Santa Paws had run so fast that there was no chance that Gregory or Timmy's brother —

whose name turned out to be Jeff — would have been able to keep up with him. The dog found himself in an overgrown vacant lot near the Oceanport VFW Hall, utterly stumped about where to go next.

According to Oceanport legend, a proud Victorian house had once stood on that exact spot during the 19th Century. It had been built by a famous sea captain who might also have been a pirate. His carpentry skills must not have been very good, though, because the house had been destroyed by a rather mild hurricane many years before. Now, all that was left were some crumbling remains. The lot was supposed to be off-limits to any trespassers, but people had been exploring the lot for years, hoping to find any gold or treasure the pirate might have left behind. But, the most exciting thing anyone had ever recovered was a dented old spoon.

Confused by the piles of snow, decayed wood, and other debris, the dog stayed where he was. He barked twice, and waited to see if there was a response. Nothing happened, so he tried again. This time, he heard the faint cry of a little boy yelling "Help!" from somewhere deep in the ground.

Yay! He had found the person who needed him! The dog picked his way carefully across what was left of the house's foundation, tracking the direction of the sound. He kept slipping in the melting snow, and once he banged his paw very hard on what must have been part of a chimney once. It hurt, and he had to limp for a few steps until the stinging stopped.

Finally, he came to a tangle of bushes, with broken branches strewn everywhere. Timmy, and his brother Jeff, had been playing a very dangerous game of hide-and-seek in the vacant lot. Timmy had ended up hiding so well that Jeff couldn't find him at all, until his brother started crying for help. That was when he had discovered what happened, and went to get some assistance from the great Santa Paws.

The dog poked through the bushes until the ground suddenly disappeared right in front of him! The dog yelped, feeling his front legs sliding into a mysterious hole. By digging his back paws firmly into the slushy ground, he managed to get his balance and stay on his feet. Then, much more cautiously, he examined the hole by walking in a wide circle around it. Once he was sure he knew where the edges were, he barked again.

"Is that Santa Paws?" a boy's voice asked weakly. He sounded very scared, and far away!

The dog barked an encouraging bark. It was hard to see into such a dark pit, but the dog was sure that the boy was in there somewhere.

"Save me, Santa Paws!" the boy begged. "I'm scared down here."

The dog thought about jumping into the hole after him, but then, how would he get out again? He was a very good jumper, but not *that* good. He would need to go get some nice people to help him. He barked again, and then started retracing his steps back across the treacherous ground.

"Wait, Santa Paws!" the boy said, his voice frantic. "Don't leave me!"

The dog did not like to hear anyone sound that frightened, and he stopped indecisively. But then, he was very happy to see Gregory and Timmy's brother Jeff rushing up to the vacant lot. And Gregory had a rope! Good! He was very, very smart about things like that.

"You guys picked *here* to come play?" Gregory said to Jeff, trying to get his breath. They had run the entire way over here. "That was pretty stupid." Although actually, he and his friend Oscar had snuck onto this vacant lot a few times themselves when they were in the fifth grade. His parents found out somehow, and he had had his television and computer privileges taken away for an entire week. The punishment must have worked, because he had never had any interest in coming back to the lot ever again. In fact, this was the first time he had set foot in there since he was ten years old. With luck, this time, his parents wouldn't be upset when they heard about it.

"We were just playing," Jeff said defensively.

"We didn't know there was an old well here or anything."

It took a few minutes for them to make their way safely over to where Santa Paws was waiting. Gregory fell twice, and manage to rip two separate holes in his jeans. Naturally, he also got wet and muddy.

Santa Paws led them to the well, and then stood protectively in front of Gregory's legs to make sure that he didn't get too close.

"We're here, Timmy," Jeff called. "We're going to get you out of there."

"Please hurry, Jeff," Timmy answered, with his voice echoing from the bottom of the well. "It's scary down here."

"Don't worry, it's going to be okay now," Jeff said confidently. "Santa Paws came, and *he'll* know what to do."

Gregory bent over to try and see inside the well. One of his basketball sneakers lost traction in the slush, and he might have tumbled down there himself, if Santa Paws hadn't instantly muscled him back to safety.

Gregory patted him, double-checked to make sure that he was standing on good, solid ground this time, and then leaned over again. It would have been much easier if he had thought to bring a flashlight along. But as far as he could tell, the well was about twenty feet deep. It might have been twenty-five feet, but probably not much more than that. Either way, it was still a long way to fall.

"Hey, Timmy," he said. "Are you hurt or anything?"

"I-I don't think so," Timmy said, but he didn't exactly sound sure of himself. His teeth were chattering, too, partially because he was chilly, and also because he was scared.

The bottom of the well was covered with thick mud, and there was also about a foot and a half of icy water that had collected in there from the melting snow. That had cushioned his fall, but the longer he was down there, the more numb and cold he felt.

"How deep is the water?" Gregory asked, when he heard splashing.

Timmy explained that his legs were stuck in the mud all the way to his knees, and the water was up past his waist, and that he *really* wanted to get out of there, *now*, because it was freezing, and it was dark, and he didn't like it.

The only problem was that Gregory knew that you weren't supposed to move people who had been injured unless you were absolutely *sure* that you wouldn't make their injuries worse. On the other hand, wouldn't Timmy know if he was seriously hurt?

"How old is he again?" he asked Jeff.

"Eight," Jeff answered. "Two weeks ago."

Then he looked shy. "I'm going to be ten in February."

"Good," Gregory said automatically. "I mean, um, happy birthday." He couldn't quite make up his mind about whether eight was old enough to understand about injuries, and he knew that there was really only one thing to do, if he wanted to be sure.

He would have to go down inside the well to find out for himself!

5

Gregory had taken a rock-climbing course the summer before, when the Callahans had gone up to New Hampshire on vacation. So he knew how to tie knots and make himself an improvised climbing harness. It wasn't perfect, but it would keep him from falling.

He used the other end of the rope to tie a canine version of the same harness around Santa Paws.

"You going to help me right, boy?" he asked.

The dog barked, knowing exactly how ropes worked and what he was supposed to do. He was nervous when he saw that Gregory was planning to go into that scary pit, but he slowly backed away to keep the rope tight.

Gregory tried to be careful as he lowered himself into the well, but he rappelled a little too quickly and landed with a loud splash. Luckily, he managed not to land on Timmy, but the well was so narrow that it was a pretty tight fit.

"Hi," Gregory said, out of breath. His boots had gone completely under the layer of mud, and he took turns yanking each one free, so that he wouldn't get stuck, too. It was pretty dark, but there was enough light so that he could see that they were, indeed, about twenty feet down, and that the little boy was standing up in the water. He was shaking from being in the water for so long, but he seemed to be okay, otherwise.

Timmy was very surprised to see a tall teenager appear next to him in the water. He had been expecting Santa Paws to leap down into the well himself. "W-what about Santa Paws?" he wanted to know, his teeth chattering even harder. "Isn't he going to save me?"

"He's going to pull us out," Gregory said. "But it might not be a good idea to move you until the rescue squad gets here. You know, so you don't get hurt."

"I'm not hurt," Timmy insisted. "I'm just really, really cold."

The rope tightened unexpectedly, and Gregory knew that Santa Paws was already trying to perform the rescue.

"Not yet, boy!" he yelled. "Stay, okay?"

The rope instantly went slack, and Gregory thought — for at least the ten thousandth time during the past few years — about what an incredibly good dog Santa Paws was. "Did you hit

49

your head, Timmy?" he asked. "Or your neck or your back or anything?"

Timmy shook his head. "No. I just fell in the mud. My knee hurts a little."

Gregory still wasn't sure how to handle this. It would be terrible to make a mistake about something so potentially serious.

"Look, see?" Before Gregory could tell him not to do it, Timmy swivelled in one direction, and then another. "I'm fine. I'm just, you know, *stuck*. I was trying to climb out before, but I kept sliding down."

Could a badly injured person climb? Probably not. Gregory slowly started untying his harness. The way he was shivering, if Timmy stayed down here much longer, he was going to get hypothermia, and then he might even go into shock or something. He knew Patricia had called "911," but she didn't know exactly where they were, so that would have made it hard to give accurate directions.

"Jeff, go out to the street and see if you can wave a car down," he shouted up to the surface. "Ask them to call the fire department for us."

Jeff hurried out to the street corner. So far, he couldn't see any cars, but he waved his arms, anyway, just in case.

Mr. Callahan and Patricia had been driving around in the general area, looking for them without success. The only clue they had was the

50

direction in which Santa Paws had been running. But then, Patricia caught sight of Jeff jumping up and down a couple of blocks away.

She pointed. "Right there, Dad. They must be in the vacant lot."

Mr. Callahan steered slowly in that direction, since the little boy seemed to be so frantic that he might forget and run out into the street. He parked the car and then used his cell phone to call the police station. To avoid any more Timmy and Lassie jokes, he asked to be connected directly to his brother Steve, and quickly reported the correct location.

Down in the well, Gregory had finally decided that it was more risky to allow Timmy to stay in the cold water than it was to have Santa Paws pull him out. So, he untied his harness, and fastened a makeshift one onto Timmy, instead.

"If anything hurts, even a little, you have to tell me right away," he warned.

Timmy thought about that, and then raised his hand timidly.

Gregory instantly stopped what he was doing. "What's wrong?"

"My throat maybe hurts," Timmy said. "Because I've been yelling so much."

"Okay," Gregory said, and couldn't help grinning. "Thanks for letting me know."

He finished tying the harness, and checked three times to make sure that the knots were nice and tight. Then he gave the rope a sharp tug.

"Okay, Santa Paws!" he called. "You can pull now."

Santa Paws started walking forward until the rope was taut. Whatever was on the other end seemed to be jammed, so he pulled steadily, but gently.

Down in the well, Gregory was trying to help pull Timmy out of the mud. He suddenly popped free, as his feet came right out of his sneakers, and Gregory was covered with a shower of mud and water.

"We're all set, Santa Paws!" he yelled towards the top of the well.

Feeling the tension of the rope change, Santa Paws pulled more industriously. It was much easier now, and he was able to walk ahead without much trouble. Whatever was down there didn't seem to weigh very much.

Patricia and Mr. Callahan, and Jeff, hurried into the vacant lot just in time to see Santa Paws hauling a muddy little boy safely out of the well.

"Good dog, Santa Paws," Mr. Callahan praised him.

Mr. Callahan thought he was good! The dog wagged his tail.

"Boy, the firefighters are going to be disappointed," Patricia said. "They hate missing out on this stuff."

The boy was obviously badly chilled and Mr. Callahan quickly untied the rope harness. Then he took off his sweater and draped it over the boy's shoulders.

Patricia looked around at the vacant lot. "So, wait. Where's Gregory?"

"Down here," Gregory said, from deep inside the well.

Patricia and Mr. Callahan were both startled to hear his voice coming from someplace right beneath them.

"You mean, you fell in, too?" Mr. Callahan asked incredulously. "Are you all right, Greg?"

"I didn't fall in," Gregory said. "I climbed down. Is Timmy all right?"

Timmy certainly seemed to be fine, but they were all glad to hear sirens, since that meant that the rescue squads would show up in a minute or two.

Patricia dropped the end of the rope to Gregory, who quickly knotted it around his waist. With Mr. Callahan and Patricia pitching in, Santa Paws was able to pull him up to safety in no time.

"Thanks," Gregory said. He tried to wipe some of the mud from his jeans and sweatshirt, but only smeared it even more badly. "Boy, this stuff smells terrible. There's all this mildew and stuff down there. Yuck."

Two police cars, a fire truck, and an ambulance

all arrived together. The paramedics swiftly examined Timmy, and announced that he seemed unharmed, but that they would take him to the hospital for a check-up, anyway. Jeff was going to ride along, too, and their parents would be at the Emergency Room waiting for them.

"So, I guess you were down there for a while," Officer Bronkowski said to Gregory, after surveying his muddy hair and disheveled clothes.

Gregory nodded, as he took the rope off Santa Paws and gave his dog a fond pat. The dog licked his hand in return.

"Find any gold or treasure?" she asked.

Gregory laughed, and shook his head. "Sorry. Just mud."

"Too bad," she said, and went to help her partner, Officer Lee, secure the area with crime scene tape.

Someone would be assigned to guard the vacant lot until one of the local construction companies could be hired to come over right away and fill the well in with dirt. That way, there would be no danger of anyone ever falling down there again.

As the ranking officer on the scene, Uncle Steve came over to take an official report. It was always funny to see Mr. Callahan and Uncle Steve standing next to each other, because they looked so much alike, but acted completely different. They were both very tall with dark hair, and a little bit of grey sprinkled in, but Mr. Callahan was always slouching and Uncle Steve was so muscular and fit that he seemed to have appeared straight from his latest workout at the gym. Also, Uncle Steve wore contact lenses, instead of glasses.

"So," he said, trying to keep a straight face. "Timmy fell down the well."

Gregory, Patricia, and Mr. Callahan all nodded.

"And Gregory got rope," Uncle Steve went on. They nodded.

"And Santa Paws saved them," Uncle Steve finished.

They nodded.

"Okay, then, that should do it." Uncle Steve wrote all of this down in his log book, then gave them a wink, and walked away.

"So, what do you think?" Patricia asked. "Front page tomorrow in the *Oceanport Oracle*, or just the lead story in the Metro section?"

"Front page," Gregory said. "And it might even make the *Boston Globe*."

"Above the fold," Mr. Callahan agreed.

Once they got home, Gregory went straight upstairs to take a shower and dump his clothes in the laundry basket. Mr. Callahan started neatly coiling up the rope, since it was a pretty safe bet that they would need it again sometime soon, and Patricia gave Santa Paws two Milk-Bones.

The dog wagged his tail and flopped down to eat his snack. He had had a very nice time in that strange backyard, but it was nice to be home again.

Hearing all of the commotion, Mrs. Callahan came out from the pantry, where she had been sorting through various canned goods.

"I was wondering where all of you had gone," she said. "Anything interesting happen?"

Mr. Callahan and Patricia looked at each other and laughed.

"Nope," Patricia said. "Same old thing."

Right after dinner, it was time to go to the park to look at the exhibits and maybe watch part of the Ice Sculpture Contest. But it was still warm and it had started to drizzle, so they were all wearing slickers instead of winter jackets. Even Santa Paws had on his specially-fitted green waterproof coat.

Uncle Steve would be off duty by now, so they were going to meet him, along with their Aunt Emily, and their cousins, Miranda and Lucy, in front of the booth sponsored by the Oceanport Brazilian Consortium. It was devoted to the history of Brazil's version of Saint Nicholas, known as *Papai Noel*. They might be serving a specially marinated Christmas turkey dish, *Ceia de Natal*, too.

Gregory and Patricia were also hoping that

they would see some of their friends at the park. They were both still feeling pretty dazed about the prospect of leaving in a few weeks, and wanted to be able to spend as much time together as possible until then.

As they walked through the crowded park, most of the people they passed said hello, but *no one* missed a chance to greet Santa Paws. Among other things, he received many compliments about how handsome he looked in his shiny green raincoat.

Uncle Steve and Aunt Emily were already in front of the *Papai Noel* booth when the Callahans got there. Since Aunt Emily worked full-time as an advertising executive in Boston, and was also raising two small children, she always looked somewhat frazzled, and tonight was no exception.

"Hi, Gregory! Hi, Patricia!" Miranda shrieked happily. "Hi, Santa Paws!"

Her little sister Lucy, who was almost two, mimicked the exact same greeting, although her pronunciation was a little fuzzy. Both girls were wearing red dresses and red rubber boots underneath their raincoats, and they looked very festive, indeed.

"I am going to be five on Wednesday," Miranda announced to everyone within hearing. Since her voice was quite piercing, that actually worked out to be a very large group of people. "I would like the new Barbie with the *pink* outfit, not the Barbie with the motor car."

Gregory nodded gravely. "Okay. Let me make sure I have this right. You want the Barbie with the blue dress, and the purple sneakers, and if possible, you'd like me to buy a car for her to drive, too."

Miranda thought that was completely hilarious, and she laughed so hard that she had to grab on to her mother's hand to keep from falling over.

The Brazilian booth was situated right between the exhibits celebrating the well-known African-American holiday, Kwanzaa, and a booth devoted to Greenland and some of its special traditions. Many people thought that Greenlanders liked to be described as Eskimos or Inuit people, but they actually far preferred to be known as *Kalaallit*. The word "Eskimo" was considered very outdated, and sometimes even offensive.

There was a woman standing in front of the booth, looking overheated in her classic Inuit parka and thick trousers. She was holding out a large tray of local delicacies.

"*Juullimi Ukiortaassamilu Pilluarit!*" she said, which was "Merry Christmas" in Greenlandic. "Would you like to try some?"

The treats looked slightly ominous, but Gregory and Patricia were too polite to say no, and they each helped themselves to one of the samples.

"That's *mattak* and *kiviak*," the woman explained. Mattak was a form of blubber, while kiviak was auk meat. "Do you like them?"

They both nodded so enthusiastically that it was clear they were not being entirely honest.

"I don't like them much, either," the woman admitted, with a grin. "But, they were extremely popular where I grew up."

"Um, it was very — chewy," Gregory said, once he had managed to swallow his.

"Do you think your dog would like some?" the woman asked.

They had never seen Santa Paws refuse *any* food, so Patricia thanked her and held out a little piece of *mattak*.

The dog sniffed it curiously, and then started chewing, and chewing, and *chewing*. He finally swallowed, blinked a few times, and then raised his right paw in his own version of being polite.

The woman laughed. "Here," she said, and handed them two pieces of candy from another plate. "I also make excellent fudge."

Gregory and Patricia ate *those* happily.

"Mom, is it okay if we walk around for a while?" Patricia asked. "See if we can find Rachel and Oscar and everyone?"

Mrs. Callahan nodded, already deep in conversation with Aunt Emily about a mystery novel they had both read recently.

The dog was following Gregory and Patricia through the crowds when he felt a tingle run along his spine. He stopped, the fur rising slightly on his back.

"Oh, no," Patricia said, recognizing the signs of an impending problem. "Here we go again."

The dog stood there, quivering, and then, galloped away from them.

There was trouble in town!

6

The dog ran out of the park, across Ocean Road, and straight towards the seawall. It was high tide, and the waves were crashing up against the rocks. Normally, he liked to stop and smell the salty air, but he didn't have time for that right now.

Three local hoodlums, Michael Smith, and Luke and Rich Crandall, had been taking turns daring each other to walk out as far as they could on the slippery rocks. The dog had run into Michael and the Crandalls many times before over the years. He had caught them shoplifting, and vandalizing cars, and once they had even tried to steal the little Baby Jesus figurine from the Nativity Scene at the Festival of Many Lands! They were all nineteen years old, but they were still in high school because they always skipped their classes and flunked their tests.

This time, however, the boys were in real trouble. None of them were very good swimmers, but that didn't stop them from taking risky chances by climbing on the algae-covered rocks. Luke had already fallen into the ocean, and when Michael tried to pull him out, he slipped in right after him. Rich had decided that he would save them, but it wasn't until he was diving in that he remembered that he could barely tread water. He not only couldn't save his brother and his friend — he wouldn't even be able to save himself!

The rain was coming down harder, and the sea was very rough. Santa Paws *did not* want to jump in there, but he had no choice. If he didn't hurry, the boys would all drown!

The dog took a running start and launched himself off a tall rock and into the water. It was cold! Really cold! Ouch!

Rich was just a few feet away, screaming for help. The dog swam over to him, and grabbed his jacket collar between his teeth. Then, he swam back to the rocks, towing Rich after him. Rich grabbed onto the closest rock and hung on for dear life.

The dog waited until he saw Rich pull himself up out of the water, and flop onto the rocks, and then he swam out after the other two boys. They might have made a very foolish mistake, but they still needed to be rescued!

* * *

Up on Ocean Road, Gregory and Patricia had no idea where their dog had gone. Oscar, as well as two of Gregory's friends from the basketball team, Abdul and Jethro, had joined them along the way, but none of them had been able to see Santa Paws clearly through the pouring rain. Actually, it was raining so hard that it was difficult to see anything at all.

"You need a tracking system for him," Oscar advised. "Sort of a Dog-Lojack idea." Even though his mother was a graphics designer and his father was a professor of music theory at Oceanport Community College, Oscar's main academic interest was science. He particularly loved gadgets. *All* gadgets.

"Any kind of GPS technology would work," Abdul said, since he liked thinking about electronics, too. "You could rig it up on his collar somehow."

Patricia sometimes got very tired of what she considered Little-Boys-and-Their-Many-Toys Syndrome. "That's great and all, guys, but it's not going to help us find him this time," she said. "So maybe we need to be kind of, you know, *practical?*"

"Let's split up," Gregory suggested. "We can cover a lot more ground that way."

Everyone seemed to think that was a good plan, and they all headed off in different directions, promising to yell if they saw Santa Paws

— or anything that looked like the sort of danger that might attract him.

Out in the water, the dog was getting tired, but he managed to reach Michael, who had just gone under for the second time. The dog grabbed his sleeve with his teeth and yanked him back up to the surface. Michael had never liked Santa Paws, and even though he didn't want to drown, he wasn't very happy when he recognized his rescuer.

"You stupid dog," he said, as he coughed and spit out seawater. "You always have to be a big, dumb hero, right?"

The dog wasn't sure what Michael was saying, but he definitely didn't like his tone of voice. He growled, but made sure not to let his teeth slip off Michael's sleeve in the process. Then he swam him back over to the rocks, where Rich was waiting and shivering.

With Rich pulling on his arms, and Santa Paws using his head to push from behind, they managed to heave Michael out of the water. In spite of himself, Michael was very grateful to be alive.

"Thanks," he muttered.

The dog growled again, and turned to go after Luke. During the time it had taken to rescue the other two, the undertow had been dragging Luke out to sea. The dog swam as hard as he could, but he couldn't seem to catch up to the current. He almost *never* had to do three rescues in a row, and the combination of the rain, and the freezing water, and the churning surf was exhausting.

Suddenly out of energy, the dog stopped swimming for a minute. It would be so easy just to swim back to the rocks by himself — or even to close his eyes and just float for a while. He almost felt like sleeping. But just as he let his head slip under the water, he felt something *different*. Something powerful. It was almost as though someone was trying to help him, and the dog thrashed his way to the surface to see who it was. He dog-paddled in place, but there was no one else there.

The dog thought that was very confusing, but he was feeling much stronger for some reason, and he surged towards the barely conscious Luke. This time, he was not going to give up until he saved him!

Up on the seawall, Gregory and Oscar were peering out at the water.

"I don't think he's there," Gregory said. "I mean, what kind of idiot would have gone swimming in the middle of winter in a rainstorm?"

Oscar pointed at two familiar figures slumped over on the rocks below them, wet and unhappy and shivering. "How about *those* two idiots?"

Gregory wiped his sleeve across his eyes so that he would be able to see better through the rain. When he realized that it was Michael Smith and Rich Crandall, he sighed.

"Figures," he said. "They're the only ones in town who would pull anything like that." Then he cupped his hands around his mouth. "Hey, Patricia! Abdul! Jethro! Over here!"

As they ran towards him, Gregory had an awful thought.

"So, if those two are down there," he said to Oscar, "where's *Luke*?" Before he could finish asking the question, he knew where Luke must be — and who was out there in the ocean trying to rescue him.

While Jethro ran to summon help, the rest of them climbed over the seawall. Rich and Michael were lying on their backs in the middle of the wet rocks, gasping for air and trying to recover from their watery ordeal.

"Are you guys all right?" Patricia asked. She actually knew them pretty well, from seeing them skulk around the halls at the high school.

Even though they were shivering, they both managed to nod sulkily.

Every few seconds, a new wave would smash against the rocks, and cover all of them with the cold spray. Gregory gulped, not wanting to imagine his dog out there somewhere in the middle of all that.

"Did Santa Paws go out to try and save Luke?" he asked.

"Like a big show-off, yeah," Michael mumbled.

Patricia quickly grabbed her brother's arm, before he could react. She knew that Gregory wanted to smack Michael — mostly because she wanted to do it, too.

"Let's just start calling him, Gregory," she said. "Let him know we're here."

The dog was only a couple of feet away from reaching Luke when he heard voices shouting his name. It was Gregory and Patricia! And their friends! Yay! But he remembered that he needed to keep swimming, before it was too late to save his third victim.

Luke's head was underwater, and Santa Paws had to sink his teeth into the boy's jeans' leg to pull him up. Gallons of heavy water had soaked into his clothes, and Luke was kind of pudgy, anyway, so it took a tremendous effort to drag him through the surf. Somehow, though, the dog still felt strong, and powerful, and he concentrated on swimming towards the voices encouraging him.

Hearing Gregory and Patricia, and thinking about how much he loved them, gave the dog *more* than enough energy to make his way back towards the shoreline.

Jethro had run into the crowded park, yelling that Santa Paws needed help right away. Immediately, half of the *town* began sprinting towards the seawall. Uncle Steve and one of his rookies, Officer Ramirez, were the first two to get there. Uncle Steve reached for his flashlight, and then remembered that he was out of uniform.

"Give them some light, okay, Roberto?" he said. "Let's get a look at what's going on down there."

Officer Ramirez fumbled for his official duty flashlight and shined it out at the ocean. Two other members of the department, who had been working crowd control, quickly added their beams to his.

As a result, hundreds of people were able to watch the dramatic conclusion to the rescues. They stood, in the pouring rain, as Santa Paws — very visible in his green raincoat — bravely dragged a limp body over to the jagged rocks. But then, a huge wave loomed up over him, and Santa Paws disappeared underneath it when it crashed down!

The entire crowd gasped in unison, and many people covered their children's eyes, while others began to weep. It would just be too horrifying to see something tragic happen to their beloved local hero, Santa Paws.

The mammoth wave ebbed away, and everyone watched anxiously to see if the courageous dog would reappear.

"Oh, this is horrid!" a voice cried through the

rain. "Someone has to go out there and save *him*."

There was a general sense of agreement among the crowd, and Uncle Steve had to take charge, before they all started climbing over the seawall simultaneously.

"Everyone, just stay where you are, please," he said in his most commanding voice. "It's not safe on those rocks. Let's wait for the rescue squad to — "

Just then, a distinctive brown furry head rose above the water. It was Santa Paws, still clutching Luke's pants leg between his teeth!

The crowd erupted into cheers.

The dog's legs were weakening from his strenuous efforts, but he was able to swim the last few feet to the rocks. Uncle Steve and Officer Ramirez lugged Luke up out of the water, while Gregory and Patricia concentrated on pulling their dog back onto dry land, where he belonged. His green raincoat was all tangled around his neck and legs, and they quickly unfastened the snaps and took it off him.

The dog felt faint from exertion, but he stood up unsteadily. Then, he shook most of the water from his coat and sneezed.

The crowd applauded wildly.

"Hooray for Santa Paws!" someone yelled.

"Our hero!" another person chimed in.

Then, as it began to sink in that Luke hadn't moved yet, the crowd fell silent again. Uncle Steve was already doing CPR, and two paramedics, Fran Minelli and Saul Rubin, were scrambling over the seawall to assist him. The situation looked very dire.

Even with the rain and waves pounding all around them, it seemed quiet. So, when Luke finally began coughing and trying to sit up, the crowd broke out into its biggest cheer yet. They clapped as Luke, Rich, and Michael were all strapped onto stretchers and carried up to waiting ambulances. They clapped some more as Uncle Steve and Officer Ramirez and Gregory's friends came over the wall and stood on the sidewalk.

But, they saved their most heartfelt applause for Santa Paws, as he jumped gracefully over the seawall, with Gregory and Patricia right behind him. Dr. Kasanofsky had been enjoying the Festival of Many Lands with his family, and he stepped forward with a stethoscope he had borrowed from one of the paramedics. He bent down to listen to the dog's heart, and then gave everyone a big thumbs-up. Santa Paws would need to have a full examination, but it was clear that he was going to be just fine.

Now, the cheers and applause were downright thunderous.

"You're a miracle, Santa Paws!" someone shouted. "What would we ever do without you?"

A pensive silence fell as everyone remembered that soon, they *would* have to do without Santa Paws. He was going to move to New York, and they would all be on their own. What were they going to do? How would they ever survive? Almost everyone bowed their heads, not wanting to imagine what life in Oceanport was going to be like from now on.

Mr. Callahan had gone off to get the car, and the crowd parted respectfully to let his station wagon through. Dr. Kasanofsky gave his keys to his wife, so that she would be able to take their children home, while he accompanied the Callahans and Santa Paws over to his office. One of his assistants had already gone ahead of them, to open the building, turn on the lights, and get the heat going. After so much time in the freezing water, Santa Paws was going to be very cold!

Gregory and Patricia rode in the far back of the car, so that Dr. Kasanofsky would have room to sit next to Santa Paws in the backseat. He kept assuring them that their dog was going to be okay, but they couldn't help worrying.

"We're going to put a warming blanket on him," Dr. Kasanofsky said, "and maybe give him some fluids, and — trust me, guys. He's *fine*."

Gregory and Patricia decided to believe him,

especially since Santa Paws had just climbed down to dig out a tennis ball from underneath the passenger's side seat. Then he settled across the backseat and started chewing.

"Well," Mrs. Callahan said, and let out her breath. "It's certainly been quite an evening, hasn't it?"

There was no way to disagree with that, so they all nodded.

"You know," Gregory said, as they drove along. "Someday, we're going to go out in public with Santa Paws, and *nothing* interesting will happen at all."

Everyone else laughed. It was hard to be sure of anything in life, but they all were pretty confident about one thing.

Being around Santa Paws was *never* going to be dull.

7

The next day was Sunday, and Santa Paws had a busy schedule. Much to Mr. and Mrs. Callahan's dismay, the family received regular requests for Santa Paws to make various public appearances. In the last week alone, he had spent an afternoon at the mall greeting small children who wanted to have a chance to sit next to Santa Paws in a big sleigh, he had been taken to Miranda's nursery school for show-and-tell, and he had also been the Guest of Honor at a big function for the Oceanport Animal Rescue League's Pet Adoption Day. After being reminded that the great Santa Paws himself had once been an abandoned stray, at least eighty families in the area promptly volunteered to fill out pet adoption questionnaires, and hundreds of other people wrote large donation checks.

Since he had passed his veterinary exam with flying colors the night before and woken up feeling perfectly fine, they decided not to cancel the activities they had already planned for the afternoon. Santa Paws was a trained Pet Therapy dog, and the Callahans brought him over to the local hospital and nursing home regularly. Today, they had hour-long visits scheduled at each facility, and it would be a shame to disappoint the people who were eagerly awaiting his appearance.

Evelyn did not like going out, so she was always allowed to stay home and relax. Abigail, however, despite her tendency to have a bad attitude, had actually managed to pass a rigorous behavior exam and become certified as a Pet Therapy cat. So she came along sometimes, depending upon whether she was in the mood.

Patricia had found a foolproof way to gauge Abigail's charitable impulses on any given day. They would set her cat carrier down on the floor in the kitchen, with the door open. If Abigail examined it with interest — sometimes she would even go inside, unasked! — then, she was willing to cooperate and make some visits. If she saw the carrier, and then hissed, or ran away, or made a point of breaking something, they knew that she had decided that her schedule was too crowded with naps and snacking to do any Pet Therapy.

On visiting days, Santa Paws always had to have a bath, and get his nails clipped. Gregory and Patricia would even brush his teeth. It was important to make sure that he was as clean as possible, since hospital administrators had a tendency to get very nervous about any possibility of spreading germs.

While Santa Paws had his bath that morning, Abigail lounged on the sink to watch. It was fun to see him look so wet and resigned and patient! When she moved over to the edge of the tub to get a better view, Gregory and Patricia knew at once that she was agreeing to be taken along on the visits today. Otherwise — since she was going to have to be bathed, too — she would have taken one look at the bathtub, and then disappeared into one of the open boxes still spread out all over in the house.

After Santa Paws had finished his bath and was wrapped up in a big, warm towel to get dry, he sat on the bath mat to admire the sight of *Abigail* in the tub. She was always very vocal, and did lots of splashing, too.

Mr. Callahan poked his head into the room as the meows and yowls got louder and louder. However, all he saw was Abigail standing placidly in the water as Gregory rubbed cat shampoo into her fur and Patricia rinsed it away. Abigail never stopped complaining the entire time, but she spoiled the effect by pausing to yawn and stretch every so often.

"She's a bit of a drama queen, isn't she," Mr. Callahan remarked.

"She's the *Queen* of the drama queens," Patricia said, as she lifted her out of the bathtub to dry her off. Abigail always enjoyed the pampering of a fluffy towel and would hold out each paw in turn to make sure all of the water was carefully removed from between her toes.

"Are you coming with us today, Dad?" Gregory asked.

Mr. Callahan shook his head. "I'm a little tired, so I'm going to take it easy. Your mother's going to go."

Patricia looked up quickly. "But, I still get to drive, right?"

Mr. Callahan smiled at her. "As far as I'm concerned, yes. But you'll have to check with her on that one."

Mr. Callahan tended to be a very easygoing front-seat supervisor, while Mrs. Callahan usually got tense and started asking things like when Patricia was going to use the brake, even if they were still a block away from a stop sign or traffic signal. Sometimes she asked if Patricia was going to brake even when the light was green!

By one-thirty, they were ready to go. Mrs. Callahan had just hung up from their daily call to check on Aunt Laurel. Actually, they usually spoke more often than that, but Mrs. Callahan *always* called at least once. Gregory and Patricia were still nervous about the upcoming move, but every time they called, Pedro and Kate sounded more and more excited by the idea — and Aunt Laurel was beginning to admit, reluctantly, that she would be very relieved to see them when they arrived. They had all talked about the three of them coming up to spend Christmas in Ocean-port, but unfortunately, Aunt Laurel wasn't well enough to travel comfortably yet. But she had lots of friends in the city, and between that, and Thelma's baby-sitting, and the visiting nurse who came by on weekdays, they would be okay for now.

Santa Paws was all suited up in his official Pet Therapy bandanna and harness, and Gregory was going to bring along a Santa Claus hat, too. People loved to see him wearing it during the holidays, and the dog didn't mind as long as it was only for an hour or two at a time.

Abigail would consent to no such foolishness of any sort, but she did allow Mrs. Callahan to tie a tiny red velvet bow onto her collar. She also voluntarily got into her carrier and only hissed twice.

Their first stop was the Seaside Nursing Home. Patricia had never driven with windshield wipers before, and she found it a tiny bit difficult to ignore them and just look at the road. Mrs. Callahan was mostly able to keep from com-menting, but her right foot would automatically pound against the car floor every so often, and

77

Patricia would take that as a cue that she should put on the brake.

The visit to the nursing home was fairly quiet, because most of the residents had gathered in the common room to watch two local actors, the Havershams, and their excessively precocious son Nathanial, do a dramatic reading from *Hedda Gabler*. As an encore, they had prepared stirring scenes from *Peer Gynt* and *Ghosts*. The Havershams were very nice people, but occasionally, when deeply moved by the beauty of their own performances, they were brought to tears, right during the middle of the show.

So, the Callahans stuck to short visits in each of the rooms which were still occupied. Santa Paws was happy to see everyone, but Abigail sometimes did nothing more than come out of her carrier, yawn, and retreat back inside.

"This doesn't really come naturally to her, does it?" a man named Mr. Layden asked when she enacted that particular stunt at the foot of his bed.

Mrs. Callahan flushed, a little embarrassed by her cat's inability to cooperate. "No, I'm afraid not."

Mr. Layden just laughed, and shook the paw Santa Paws offered him. "Well, it's entertaining. I'm not sure I'd have fun seeing a cat who *enjoyed* being social."

The last room they visited was where a woman

named Mrs. Amory was staying. She was particularly fond of Santa Paws, because many years earlier, he had rescued her when she slipped on the ice and broke her hip. And this time, Abigail came out long enough to be patted, twice, on the head, before returning to her carrier.

Mrs. Amory was a very gregarious person, and Patricia was surprised to see her in her room reading a book, instead of out watching the Havershams. But she had been a newspaper journalist for many years, and she was unusually well-read, so maybe she just wasn't a fan of those particular plays.

"You didn't want to go see the Afternoon with Ibsen?" she asked curiously.

Mrs. Amory grinned. "The very idea gives me a headache." Then, she looked guilty. "It's not that they're not — well, let's just say that I find them, um, *energetic*."

The Havershams were, indeed, nothing if not energetic. Gregory and Patricia and their mother were actually privately relieved that they weren't being asked to sit through the Afternoon with Ibsen, either.

After Santa Paws stopped to have a Milk-Bone and some water in the Nurses' Break Room, they went over to Oceanport Memorial Hospital. Today, they were planning to spend most of their visit in the Pediatrics Ward. Before they went inside, Gregory held the Santa hat out and the dog moved forward to let him put it on his head. It sat there at a jaunty tilt, and Gregory had to move the pom-pom back so that it wouldn't get in his eyes.

The dog thought *all* visits were fun, but he was especially happy when he got to spend time with children. Everyone they passed in the hallways waved or paused to say hello, and the dog wagged his tail nonstop.

The Pediatrics Ward was clean and bright and filled with toys. Obviously, none of the children were happy about having to be in the hospital, especially at Christmastime, but when Santa Paws walked in, there were smiles everywhere. He moved from one bed to another, spending a little time with each child in turn. Some of the children only wanted to admire him, while others liked to hug him or have him lick their faces.

The nurses were accustomed to having Santa Paws visit, and they had learned that the best thing to do was step back and let him follow his instincts. Whenever he came, they would bring out a small basket full of plastic bones and balls, which children could throw around the room for him to fetch.

While Santa Paws was busy fetching, and barking on command, Abigail sat on top of her carrier to survey the entire room. As usual, she thought the dog was making a spectacle of himself, but that was really only to be expected with dogs. But, since the ward was filled with two long rows of beds, she thought it might be fun to jump from one to another as fast as she could.

Everyone laughed as they watched Abigail cavorting around the room. When she reached the bed on the end, she saw a *very tempting* place to go next. Two of the children had spent part of the morning building a tall and complicated stack of blocks. They had been trying to see how high they could build it without having all of the blocks fall down. Abigail eyed the pile, with her eyes gleaming wickedly. What fun it would be to balance on top of it!

Then, before anyone could stop her, she made a great leap from the bed, aiming for the top two blocks. She landed so delicately that, for a moment, it looked as though the flimsy stack might actually be able to support her weight. But then, the pile began to sway slowly from side to side. Abigail teetered on her two blocks, beginning to wonder whether this had been such a great idea, after all.

The block pile swayed to the left, swayed to the right — and then came tumbling down with a great crash! Abigail landed in the middle of the jumbled blocks, looking very surprised to find herself on the floor. Deeply embarrassed by having been clumsy, in *front* of people, she summoned what remained of her dignity and marched over to the nearest windowsill. She jumped onto

81

it, and began washing her face with great concentration.

The children laughed and clapped, since most of them thought she might have knocked over the pile on purpose. Seeing the blocks strewn everywhere, Santa Paws began picking them up in his mouth and dropping them into the basket where the nursing staff kept his dog toys. Some of the children who were well enough to get out of bed ran over eagerly to help him.

"So how come he doesn't do chores at home?" Patricia asked Gregory. "It would certainly save us a lot of time, if he did."

Gregory nodded. "I wish we could train him how to use the vacuum cleaner. I hate doing that."

"Unloading the dishwasher would be nice, too," Patricia said.

While Santa Paws was tidying up, one of the nurses took Mrs. Callahan aside.

"We're very worried about a little girl down the hall," she said. "She's been unconscious since they brought her in here a few days ago. Her parents told me she loves pets. Do you think it might help if Santa Paws and your cat went in there?"

Mrs. Callahan had no idea, but it seemed as though it would be worth a try. "Well, I don't think it could hurt," she said.

As they all walked down the hallway, they saw

a group of worried relatives huddled together outside the little girl's room. Some of them were crying, and all of them looked extremely upset. Her parents were in the room, sitting by her bedside and praying that she would come out of her coma.

The nurse went in first to let the parents know that Santa Paws was ready and waiting to come in. She reappeared a minute later.

"They'd like to see your pets, but we can only allow one extra person in there," the nurse said.

Since Gregory was the one who had faithfully gone to all of the Pet Therapy training and certification sessions, he was the obvious choice. He entered the room shyly, holding Abigail's carrier in one hand, and his dog's leash in the other. He had never visited anyone in a coma before, and he wasn't sure what it would be like.

He was surprised to find that the room didn't look bright and antiseptic the way they always did on television. The only light was a small lamp in the corner, and there were posters on the walls, stuffed animals on the bed, and a portable CD player playing some kind of pop music. Gregory wasn't a big fan of bubble-gum pop, but he knew that it was some well-known girls' band. Or maybe the singers were boys with really high voices — he wasn't quite sure. The doctors had advised the girl's parents to bring as many of her possessions as possible to the hospital. They were hoping that being surrounded by familiar objects would help her progress. But so far, she had remained in her coma.

The little girl, whose name was Nina, was lying in her hospital bed with her eyes closed. A homemade quilt was covering her. Her mother, Mrs. Schnagel, was holding her hand, while her father stood behind her. When he saw Gregory, he came over to say hello.

"I, uh, I'm sorry about this," Gregory said awkwardly.

"The doctors think it might be worth a try," Mr. Schnagel answered. "We brought her poodle in last night, but Nina didn't respond at all."

They looked at each other, uncomfortably.

"I usually take Santa Paws off his leash, and let him, you know, do what he thinks is the right thing to do," Gregory said.

Mr. and Mrs. Schnagel glanced at the nurse, who nodded. So, Gregory unhooked the leash and, after checking with the nurse, opened Abigail's carrier door, too. Then he stepped out of the way. During Pet Therapy visits, he sometimes felt like an intruder, and it almost always seemed better to keep a low profile and let Santa Paws take charge.

The dog went straight to the bed and sniffed curiously. Then he lifted his paws on the edge of the mattress. Gregory could tell that he wanted to get up there, and he looked at the nurse, who nodded that it was okay.

"Good boy," Gregory said softly. "Up."

Santa Paws jumped onto the bed very carefully and then settled down until he was lying right next to the comatose little girl. He rested his head on his shoulder, and stayed there without moving. Then, Abigail hopped onto the bed, too, and Gregory tensed, afraid of what she might do. But, moving just as gently as Santa Paws had, she simply walked along the other side of the bed and curled up on top of the girl's stomach, where she began purring.

The dog sensed that the girl needed for him to be as still and peaceful as possible. She was breathing very slowly — *too* slowly — and he timed his breathing to match hers, as Abigail purred steadily. For a second, the dog had that same strange feeling of not being alone that he had noticed the night before during his ocean rescues. It startled him, but he just concentrated on the little girl.

Gregory and the Schnagels and the nurse watched in complete silence. Mrs. Schnagel started to say something, but the nurse instantly held up her hand, and she stopped.

Slowly, gradually, patiently, the dog began to breathe a tiny bit faster, and Nina's respirations started to speed up, too. The nurse noticed this at once and took an instinctive step closer to the bed. But Nina and Santa Paws were breathing smoothly and evenly together, so she stayed where she was.

Now the dog began to make a sound Gregory had never heard before. It was sort of like purring, and almost like talking, but it wasn't, either. He would almost have described it as *singing*. Abigail's purring intensified, too, the pitch very similar to the soothing noise the dog was making.

Then, like a flash, Abigail's paw whipped up and tapped the girl lightly on the cheek. Everyone in the room either jumped or gasped, but before they had time to do anything else, something wonderful happened.

The little girl opened her eyes!

8

The little girl looked around, blinked, and looked around some more. Then, she focused directly on Santa Paws.

"Hi, doggie," she said.

Her parents both burst into tears, and Gregory kind of felt like crying, too. For all he knew, the *nurse* wanted to do some crying of her own.

Within no time, other nurses and several doctors had crowded into the room. Abigail found their excited conversation, with everyone interrupting everyone else at once, distasteful, if not downright rude, so she stamped over to her carrier for some privacy. Santa Paws trotted over to sit next to Gregory, who kissed him on top of the head.

"Good boy," he whispered.

Lying in her bed, Nina seemed bewildered, but not frightened or upset. She kept asking her parents where they were, and why all of the doctors were bothering them. She also wanted to know if she could have a hamburger, please, very soon, plain, with no ketchup or mustard, and maybe a pickle and some french fries, as long as there was *no ketchup*.

Feeling a little self-conscious about being caught in the middle of a private family moment, Gregory discreetly left the room, with Santa Paws and Abigail in tow. The joyous news had spread throughout the entire wing of the hospital, and Nina's relatives and friends were laughing and hugging each other out in the hallway.

Everyone wanted to embrace Santa Paws at the same time, and Gregory could tell that his dog was starting to feel overwhelmed.

"Thank you," he said, as politely as possible, "but my mother and sister are waiting for us, and we need to take the animals home for some supper."

The dog's ears flew up. Supper! Yay! His whole body wiggled with excitement, and he whipped his tail back and forth furiously.

Abigail's ears also flickered when she heard that word, but she had no interest in reacting in the same sort of shamefully demonstrative way.

No one wanted to do anything to prevent the great Santa Paws, and his ill-tempered feline sidekick, from having their supper on time, so they moved aside to let them move on undisturbed. Mrs. Callahan and Patricia came down the hallway to meet them, and Gregory handed his mother Abigail's carrier. Then, he gave Patricia Santa Paws' leash to hold, because — well, frankly, he was feeling a little shaky after what he had just witnessed.

"So," Patricia said. "Another day, another miracle?"

Gregory grinned. Not everyone appreciated Patricia's sense of humor, but he was a pretty big fan of irreverence, even though he wasn't very good at it himself. "Something like that," he said, "yeah."

When they got home, they found Mr. Callahan lying on the couch, waiting for the Patriots game to start. After feeding Santa Paws, Gregory immediately claimed the love seat for himself, which left Patricia with a choice between the rocking chair or the rug. She selected the rug, after grabbing a couple of pillows to put underneath her head.

Mrs. Callahan had no interest in football whatsoever — except when her son was playing; which mostly just made her anxious — so, she went upstairs with a book and a cup of hot tea. Evelyn and Abigail followed her, since they found it unpleasant to be in a room when people were yelling things like, "Go, go, go!" and "Oh, no, don't throw it away!" Santa Paws flopped down on the floor, and took a nap next to Patricia.

"He looks worn out," Mr. Callahan observed. "Did he work even harder than usual today?"

Gregory looked at Patricia, who just laughed. "Yeah," he said. "He definitely did."

Since they hadn't had enough time to see many of the exhibits, the Callahans decided to go back down to the Festival of Many Lands that night. The Ice Sculpture Contest had been rained out again, and the Oceanport Amateur Brass Band members were all afraid to take their instruments out of their cases, but other than that, the Festival was running smoothly.

They had strongly considered letting Santa Paws stay at home, so he wouldn't feel compelled to rescue anyone. But he was so crushed when he saw them leaving without him, that Mr. and Mrs. Callahan relented and allowed him to come along.

Once they got to the park, Gregory and Patricia went off with Santa Paws to meet their friends Oscar and Rachel in front of the *Chanukah or Hanukkah? Why, Both are Just Fine!* booth. Oscar was always hungry and he was busy eating some of the latkes Mrs. Gladstone, the rabbi's wife, was frying on a small portable stove.

Rachel had been Patricia's best friend since kindergarten. She was blind and had used a cane for years, but the previous summer, she had finally been old enough to be eligible to get a guide dog. She had spent several weeks at a residential training program, and had returned with an amiable Golden Retriever named Spike.

Santa Paws had never been quite sure what to make of Spike. The other dog seemed friendly enough, but he had no interest in being social. Actually, Santa Paws was generally confused by how to behave around other dogs, since he really only spent time with cats, as a rule. Except when he was rescuing them, he just didn't have much contact with Oceanport dogs. But, he wagged his tail at Spike, who wagged back, and that was that.

"*Excellent* Patriots game," Oscar said.

"Oh, yeah," Gregory said, and they exchanged high-fives. Any Patriots victory was great, but whenever they beat the Jets, it was just that much more rewarding. Pedro and Kate had been insisting on the telephone that wearing Red Sox or Patriots caps out in public in New York City was going to be looking for trouble — but Gregory had *no* intention of not supporting his teams, and Patricia felt the same way. So, they just figured that they would have to look for a little trouble.

"How's the packing nightmare?" Rachel asked.

"Nightmarish," Patricia said without hesitating. "I did a little bit more during half-time, but mostly, we were just lying around, watching the game."

"Well, I can come over and help this week,"

Rachel said. "You know, whenever you want."

Patricia nodded, trying not to feel miserable about the ever-looming reality of leaving Oceanport soon. "Yeah, that would be good. I mean, you know."

"Yeah," Rachel said, feeling just as sad as Patricia did. "At least with Spike, I can travel by myself now. So, I can come down to New York on the train, and visit and everything. It's not that far, when you think about it."

"That would be *great*," Patricia said. And, now that she thought about it, her parents would probably let her take the train up sometimes to visit Rachel and her other friends, too.

They were passing the booth put together by the Oceanport Memories of Malta Club. The banner across the top read: *"Il-Milied it-Tajjeb! Is-Sena t-Tajba!,"* which meant Merry Christmas, and Happy New Year in Maltese. They were serving cups of hot chestnut soup, called *imbuljuta*, and two men were playing a slightly out-of-tune duet of "Away in a Manger" on the bagpipes.

"Oh, this is pretty neat," Patricia said, looking at the vast array of creches in the booth. Some of them were life-sized, while others were small enough to fit in a person's hand. Each one was filled with intricate handmade figurines, representing various people and animals from the Christmas story. They had been constructed of

92

folded paper, wax, clay, molten metal, and even plastic. "There are about forty different creches in here."

"*Il-Presepju*," the woman running the booth told her. "We also call them cribs."

After asking permission, Rachel ran her fingers over some of the more sturdy cribs and figures, while Patricia described what she was touching in great detail. Over the years, they had gotten very accustomed to operating that way, and Rachel had always assured Patricia that all of that explaining would do wonders for her sense of narrative drive.

They checked out the exhibit devoted to Hong Kong, and its traditional *Ta Chiu* festival, which was held every year on December 27th. After wishing them a *Sheng Tan Kuai Loh!*, the local Taoist priest wrote all of their names — including Santa Paws and Spike — on pieces of paper. Then, he taped them to a tiny origami horse made from construction paper and lit it on fire to send their names up to the sky for a blessing from the heavens. This was traditionally a very solemn religious ceremony of renewal, but there was something very cheerful about it, too.

They didn't mind learning about different traditions, but on the whole, Gregory and Oscar were more interested in visiting the booths serving food. They tried Billy Can Pudding from Australia, *bacalhau*, which was a salted dry cod-fish dish from Portugal, slices of *christop-somo* sweet bread from Greece, an iced Sorrel drink from Jamaica, *Julegroed* Christmas porridge from Denmark, Christmas *Lebkuchen* biscuits from Egypt, chapatis, which were a type of bread from Kenya, and some Austrian cheese crêpes called *Topfenpalatschinken*.

Patricia shook her head. "Gregory, remember about an hour ago at dinner, when you ate more than the rest of us put together?"

"I'm a growing boy," Gregory said, busy with a small plate of a chicken stew called *Doro wat* and *injera* bread, from Ethiopia. "I need lots of energy."

"What you're going to need is lots of *antacids*," Rachel said.

Patricia shuddered. "Don't get him started — he's really into burping these days."

Gregory hung his head, and pretended to be shy. "I have a special gift."

"You spend too much time *practicing*," Patricia said.

It was still drizzling, but not enough to spoil anyone's fun. As they ambled along through the Festival, Santa Paws was, of course, greeted by everyone they passed. Sometimes, people insisted upon all of them stopping, so that they could take his picture. One little boy was so excited to see Santa Paws in the flesh that he burst into tears, and Santa Paws had to roll over a few times and walk on his hind legs briefly before the boy was able to pull himself together and stop crying long enough to shake his hero's paw.

At exactly nine o'clock, a huge brass bell next to the World War II memorial began to ring in long, echoing tones.

"What's that?" Rachel asked curiously.

"Everyone from the Town Council is standing over by the war memorials. Maybe they're going to have a ceremony of some kind?" Patricia guessed.

Oscar stopped eating long enough to look around. "Hey, I should find my dad. He loves stuff like that." Oscar's father had served in Vietnam, and was very active in a number of local veterans' organizations.

The entire crowd was hurrying towards the war memorials. There seemed to be a great feeling of anticipation in the air.

"Excuse me," Gregory said, as he saw Mr. Corcoran, one of his father's many friends from Sally's Diner and Sundries Shop, going by. When his father had writer's block, he often went down to the diner to drink coffee and talk about sports and politics for a couple of hours. "What's going on, sir?"

Mr. Corcoran looked at him, looked at Santa Paws, and smiled. "Didn't anyone tell you, son? You all had better come along."

They followed him towards the memorials, and

Patricia saw that her parents were also being ushered over to that section of the park. The closer they got, the more everyone else smiled at them.

A small wooden platform had been set up right between the memorials and the bandstand. The platform was decorated with red and green bunting, and there was a large object covered with a thick cloth directly in the middle of the stage. Hanging above it was what appeared to be a sign of some kind, but it was also covered. Mr. Gustave, the mayor of Oceanport, was standing on the platform, holding a microphone.

"Welcome, good citizens of Oceanport!" he said. "Could the Callahans please come forward with our beloved friend, Santa Paws?"

Gregory and Patricia looked at each other.

"Is this weird, or what?" he asked, in a low voice.

"Totally weird," she said, just as quietly.

Neither of them really liked being at the center of so much attention, and as their parents came forward, it was clear that they felt somewhat uncomfortable, too.

"Do you have any idea what's going on?" Patricia whispered.

Her mother shook her head. "No, but I'm beginning to think we probably have stayed home and watched television tonight," she whispered back.

"Could Santa Paws please come up on the stage?" Mayor Gustave asked.

Gregory looked at his father, feeling a little panicky. "We don't have to go up there *with* him, do we?"

Mr. Callahan shrugged. "Not if he'll go up there by himself."

Gregory unclipped the leash, and then pointed towards the platform. "Go, Santa Paws, okay? Up!"

The dog was perplexed, but he wanted to make Gregory happy, so he jumped onto the platform. His back foot got caught in some of the bunting, and it tore slightly as he yanked it free.

"Sit, please, Santa Paws," Mayor Gustave said.

The dog was baffled, but he sat down obediently.

Mayor Gustave motioned to two of the Town Council members, each of whom were holding one end of a gold braided rope. They both tugged the rope at the same time and the red curtain dropped away to reveal a huge brightly-painted banner at least eight feet high and twenty feet long. The banner said: "Bon Voyage, and Thank You, Santa Paws!"

The crowd began to clap and cheer, and Mayor Gustave held up his hand.

"Wait, wait," he said. "We also have some special gifts we want to present. But, first, it's time for a tune." He turned towards the bandstand, where the Oceanport A capella Choir had been waiting for their cue, and gave them an OK sign.

Their director, Mrs. Quigley, tapped her baton on her music stand and then raised her arms to conduct as the choir burst into a song that she had written herself. It was called "The Ballad of Santa Paws," and it had twenty-six verses.

They were just starting the fourteenth verse, when the dog stood up, looking urgent and alert.

"Oh, no," Mrs. Callahan said, and the rest of the family winced along with her.

The dog leaped off the platform and dashed through the crowd at top-speed.

Someone needed his help, right away!

9

On the bandstand, Mrs. Quigley was still conducting furiously, but the choir had stopped singing. She whacked her baton on the music stand, but they weren't even looking in her direction. So, she whacked harder, and finally, she banged it quite forcefully — which got the choir's full attention.

"Verse fourteen," she said in a firm voice. "From the top."

And so, meekly, the choir resumed the song.

In the meantime, the dog had long since left the park and was halfway up Main Street. Then, as he got closer to Mabel's Five-and-Dime, he slowed to a walk. There was a woman stumbling around in front of the closed store, talking rapidly to herself. She swayed on her feet, and then stumbled around some more.

"Isn't that awful," a man standing across the street said to his wife. "Getting drunk, during the ceremony for Santa Paws!"

"It's terrible," his wife agreed. "Someone should pass a law against it."

Santa Paws had never seen anyone act the way this woman was acting, and he approached her cautiously. He stopped two feet away, and barked once.

"*Dogs*," the woman said angrily, her speech slurred and indistinct. "Dogs and hogs, in bogs. Leave me alone!"

The dog knew that something must be very wrong, and he barked loudly, hoping that someone would come and help him.

Gregory and Oscar were the first ones to catch up to him.

"Hey, whoa," Gregory said, when he saw the woman lurching back and forth. "What do we do?"

Oscar was just as apprehensive. "I don't know. Where's your uncle? He's probably used to stuff like this."

The woman kept talking and talking, and then, in the middle of a sentence, toppled forward towards the sidewalk. Santa Paws jumped forward just in time to break her fall, and she landed right on top of him. It was very uncomfortable, lying pinned against the cold sidewalk, but Santa Paws didn't move, because then there would be no way to protect her from sprawling against the wet concrete herself.

Patricia was the next one to show up, out of breath from running so fast.

"What's going on?" she asked. "Did she jump on him?"

Oscar shook his head. "She fell down. We think she might have passed out."

More people had appeared now, and they stood in an uncertain circle around the barely-conscious woman.

"What do we do?" someone asked.

"We call the police," the man who had been across the street said grimly. "She's drunk as can be."

At least two dozen different people whipped out their cell phones to dial "911." But before the dispatcher's office could even answer the flurry of calls, Uncle Steve had already pulled up in his squad car with his second-in-command, Sergeant Zimmerman.

Before getting out of the car, Uncle Steve called in an immediate request for an ambulance.

"Are you on Main Street by the Five-and-Dime, Lieutenant?" the dispatcher asked, sounding very harassed. "Because we've already had at least thirty calls about it."

Uncle Steve looked around and saw cell phones everywhere. "Right. Okay," he said. "Don't send thirty ambulances."

"We don't *have* thirty ambulances," the dispatcher responded testily.

By the time two of the town's three ambulances showed up, Uncle Steve was already checking the woman's wrist for a Medic-Alert bracelet. When he found one, he nodded to himself.

"Have you eaten today, ma'am?" he asked. "Have you taken any insulin?"

The woman's response was too garbled to understand.

"Insulin," someone in the crowd said wisely. "She must be in a diabetic coma."

"Not necessarily," someone else said. "She could be in sugar shock. That's *completely* different."

As the two men argued about the difference between hypoglycemia and hy*per*glycemia, the paramedics lifted the woman off Santa Paws and put her on a gurney. Recognizing the signs of insulin shock at once, they placed a small glucose tablet underneath her tongue. Within seconds, the woman's eyes flew open.

"What's going on?" she asked. "Where am I?" She saw the huge group of people surrounding her gurney and blushed. "I'm sorry. Did I pass out?"

The contrast between the woman who had been stumbling and mumbling — and this woman who made perfect sense — was startling. It had, of course, been a purely medical emergency, and she had not had any alcohol to drink at all.

"Thank you, Santa Paws," she said weakly, as the paramedics lifted her into the ambulance.

Even after the ambulance pulled away, more people were still running over to see what had happened. Witnesses started describing, at length, the way Santa Paws had found a woman in terrible shape, immediately diagnosed her diabetic condition with his vast store of medical knowledge, and cured her completely in a matter of seconds. Two reporters who had arrived late began copying down every single word in their notebooks.

"Did I miss the part where he administered treatment and then put his paws on her and healed her?" Patricia asked Gregory.

He nodded. "Yeah. You should have run faster."

The commotion began to die down, and everyone trooped back to the park to resume the ceremony for Santa Paws. Mayor Gustave presented him with a number of gifts, including a large trophy, several blue ribbons, a box of homemade truffles, and an engraved plaque. Then, the choir sang the last twelve verses of "The Ballad of Santa Paws," as well as two other songs Mrs. Quigley had composed called "Where, oh, Where is Our Hero Tonight?" and "Hail to Santa Paws, the Canine King!"

As a grand finale, Mayor Gustave dramatically unveiled the mysterious cloth-covered object on the platform. It was a full-scale papier-mâché model of Santa Paws standing proudly on a rock,

103

apparently staring out to sea. Mayor Gustave announced that a statue had been commissioned to honor Santa Paws, to be placed in the center of the park, and that it would be an exact replica of the model they saw before them.

Unfortunately, the papier-mâché had not fared very well on such a wet evening and it was sagging in several places. In fact, the ears on the statue were drooping so low that Santa Paws looked more like a bloodhound than himself.

Even so, everyone clapped and cheered and threw damp confetti. Mrs. Quigley was eager to have the choir go through another full rendition of "The Ballad of Santa Paws," but it was getting very late and Mayor Gustave managed to convince her to save it for another evening.

Before leaving, a long line of people waited in turn to shake the dog's paw and thank him for helping them so much over the years. Some of them wept, while others just shook his paw and moved on.

When everyone else was finally gone, the Callahans stood in front of the platform, trying to absorb everything that had just happened. They were astounded, and touched, by the depth of feeling their fellow citizens had shown them tonight.

"Well, gosh," Mr. Callahan said, and gave Santa Paws a pat on the head.

The dog wagged his tail, and yawned. He had

had a very long day, and he hoped that they were going to go home soon.

The rest of them were still speechless, and they stood there in the drizzle for another minute or two, holding the vast array of gifts in their arms.

"Twenty-six verses," Patricia said finally.

They all grinned. Then, without another word, they headed for their car.

The next morning, the Callahans sat at the kitchen table, eating breakfast. This time, they were only having cereal and toast and juice, but it was still nice to be together. It was the day before Christmas Eve, and Gregory was shocked when it occurred to him that this was their very last day at Oceanport High School. Christmas Eve was the beginning of their holiday vacation, and by the time school started again, they would be busy doing their final packing and getting ready to move to New York.

"Hey, this is really it, isn't it," he said. "I mean, like, we have to say good-bye to everyone today."

Patricia had already known that, but somehow, it sounded worse to hear him actually say it aloud. She instantly lost her appetite, and had to put her spoon down before she had even taken her first bite of cereal.

"It's only temporary," Mr. Callahan reminded them. "Plus, we can come back to visit whenever you want, and we'll probably spend most of the summer here."

"So, how come you're not eating, either?" Gregory asked.

"Oh, I'm just not hungry," Mr. Callahan said. "My stomach hurts."

Mrs. Callahan leaned over to touch his forehead with the back of her hand, looking concerned. "I hope you're not coming down with anything. I'd hate to see any of us be sick on Christmas."

"It's only a stomachache," Mr. Callahan assured her. "No big deal." He gestured towards the clock on the wall. "And you all had better get moving, or you're going to be late."

"Okay," Mrs. Callahan said, as she put on her coat and picked up her briefcase. Then she kissed him good-bye. "But promise to take it easy today."

"I have to write my book," he said.

Gregory nudged Patricia. "I bet you a thousand dollars that if we woke him up in the middle of the night, that's the first thing he'd say."

Not that either of them had a thousand dollars, but that was a bet Patricia would never take — because she knew she would lose.

Once they had all left for school, Mr. Callahan went back upstairs to lie down. He really didn't feel very good, but he was pretty sure that it was because he had eaten so many exotic foods at the Festival the night before. He figured that if he read for a while, sipped some ginger ale, and then took a nap, he would be just fine.

There was a fireplace in Mr. and Mrs. Callahan's room, and the dog sat on the rug in front of it. There was no fire burning, but he wanted to be ready, in case Mr. Callahan decided to light one. It was always so nice and warm and comfortable to lie in front of a roaring fire.

Just thinking about what that would be like made the dog sleepy. So he curled up and took a nap, snoring a little.

Up on the bed, Mr. Callahan was reading a very interesting textbook about criminalistics, but no matter how hard he tried, he couldn't seem to concentrate. So, he closed the book, stretched out in bed and stared up at the ceiling. Usually he had no trouble falling asleep, but today — well, his stomach hurt. He was lying there, looking at nothing in particular, when Abigail unexpectedly landed on top of him. It was extremely painful, and he groaned.

"Abigail, don't *do* that," he said, with his teeth gritted.

Abigail did not like being spurned in such a cavalier manner, and she regally left the bed and went downstairs to sulk, and eat icicles from the Christmas tree.

After tossing and turning for a while, Mr. Callahan finally managed to fall asleep. He was sure — *absolutely sure* — that when he woke up, he would feel just fine.

Two hours later, Mr. Callahan woke up. He didn't feel fine. But he decided to go downstairs and work on his book for a while. The dog followed him, hoping that he was going to fix them a snack. Instead, all Mr. Callahan did was pour himself some more ginger ale and take a couple of aspirin.

The dog looked longingly up at the box of Milk-Bones on top of the refrigerator, wishing that he could jump that high. Abigail could get up there, by leaping from one of the counters, but he had never tried to do that himself because he knew it would be bad.

When Mr. Callahan didn't make a move to get him a biscuit, the dog went over to sit in front of the backdoor. If he couldn't have a treat, maybe it would be nice to go outside in the yard for a while. The temperature was much colder than it had been for the past few days, but it had finally stopped raining, and he could play in the frozen mud.

But Mr. Callahan left the room, without even glancing in his direction. That was very strange, and the dog followed him nervously. When he and Mr. Callahan went to the kitchen during the day, he was *always* given a Milk-Bone, and after that, he *always* went outside to run around.

In the den, Mr. Callahan sat down at his desk and turned on his computer. His stomach and side were hurting more and more, and he gave some thought to calling the doctor for advice. But he probably just had the flu, and so he didn't want to bother her. Maybe he would call later, if he started feeling worse. His face seemed very hot, and he wondered if he was running a fever. But he didn't feel well enough to walk upstairs and get the thermometer right now.

The dog sat on the floor behind him, watching with worried eyes. Mr. Callahan just didn't seem like himself at all. What could be wrong? What should he do? He wished that Gregory and Patricia and Mrs. Callahan were home, because they were very smart, and they would understand what was going on.

After staring at his computer without moving for about ten minutes, Mr. Callahan realized that it was useless to try and get any work done when he felt so lousy. So, he moved over to the couch to lie down for a while. Another nap might help, or he could listen to some Frank Sinatra CDs. The only music he *ever* listened to was Frank Sinatra, except, on very rare occasions, when he listened to Ella Fitzgerald. But right now, it felt as though it would take too much effort to turn the stereo on.

Just then, Abigail walked into the den, vomited some icicles onto the braided rug in front of him, and walked out again.

"Great," Mr. Callahan said with a sigh. "That's just great."

He pulled a few tissues from the box on the coffee table, and got up so that he could clean up the mess. But when he tried to bend over, he felt a jolt of such excruciating pain that he couldn't get his breath.

"Oh, boy," he said, and grabbed his side. He was starting to feel very dizzy, and he knew he should try to get back to the couch, or at least sit down on the rug. But the pain in his side was getting stronger, and before he could taken a single step, he fainted.

The dog stared in complete dismay as he saw Mr. Callahan starting to fall. He landed with a heavy thud, and didn't move.

There was something horribly wrong with Mr. Callahan!

10

The dog rushed over to Mr. Callahan, even though he was sure that he would get up right away. But he didn't! He just stayed there, on the floor, with his eyes closed! The dog barked several times, but Mr. Callahan didn't react at all.

Not sure what else to do, the dog used his front paw to push Mr. Callahan's shoulder. When Mr. Callahan *still* didn't move, he nudged him harder, but Mr. Callahan's eyes stayed shut. Panicking now, the dog ran back and forth on the rug, barking at the top of his lungs.

Abigail and Evelyn had heard the ominous thud from all the way upstairs, and they both came running. They knew from the frantic note in the dog's barks that something terrible was going on. But the last thing they expected to see was Mr. Callahan lying on the floor, without moving. How could something happen to Mr. Callahan? Nothing bad *ever* happened to Mr. Callahan!

By now, the dog was sitting on the floor, panting anxiously. He was too scared to think about what he should be doing, and he just panted and shivered on the rug.

Evelyn was not at all experienced when it came to rescuing people, so she just went over and curled up against Mr. Callahan's unconscious body. She pressed tightly against him and purred, to try and make him feel better.

The dog was still panting and shivering. What should he do? Why didn't his family come home and fix this? Where *were* they?

Abigail had spent many tense hours with Santa Paws over the years, but she had never seen him look so lost and frightened. The fact that Santa Paws was scared made *her* feel afraid, too. She went over to join Evelyn, adding a shaky little purr of her own.

The dog knew that he had to think. He had performed so many rescues, for so many strangers, but he had almost never had to rescue someone he *loved*. The idea of something being wrong with Mr. Callahan was so upsetting that it was hard to think about anything else. But he *had* to think. Mr. Callahan needed his help.

This wasn't Mr. Callahan; this was a rescue. If he remembered that it was a rescue, he might be less scared. What would he do if this *wasn't* one of the Callahans, who he worshiped and adored? The dog closed his eyes to try and think.

Across the room, Evelyn and Abigail got very angry when they saw his eyes close, because they were afraid he might be taking another one of his constant naps, even though this would be a *very bad* time to do that. Abigail was going to go over and whack him with her paw until he woke up, but she couldn't bear to leave Mr. Callahan's side. So she stayed where she was, sending her meanest look in the dog's direction.

The dog kept his eyes closed, and tried to breathe through his nose, instead of panting. For some reason, when he panted, that made it harder to think. But he was so scared! Then, out of nowhere, that sense of calm and safety he had had sometimes felt lately welled up inside his chest. Help. He need to find help. Whenever he came across injured people, he always went someplace to get them some help, and that's what he needed to do for Mr. Callahan.

When the dog opened his eyes, his expression was much less frantic, and the cats felt some of their own pent-up tension fade away. He looked at them, with a steady gaze, wanting to be sure that they would stay and keep Mr. Callahan company until he got back. Then he headed for the hall.

Right now, he needed to find a way out of the house!

He ran out to the kitchen and threw himself against the backdoor as hard as he could. But it didn't budge. So, he raced through the house to the front door, and tried to knock it open, only to find that it was securely locked, too.

Now what should he try? The windows! He could break the windows! Then he would be able to run outside. The dog dashed to the living room and hurled himself against the bay windows. After several tries, he managed to crack a couple of the panes, but because it was the middle of winter, there were *other* windows behind the main windows, and even if he could break through one, it would be impossible to break through *two*.

The house was full of windows, though, and he would just keep trying until he found one he could break. He ran from room to room, but there didn't seem to be any window flimsy enough for him to smash. So he sat on his haunches, and started panting again.

Air. He could smell fresh air. Where was it coming from? If there was fresh air coming in, there had to be a way to get *out* of the house. The fireplace! He rushed to the living room and knocked over the metal screen in front of the fireplace with one ferocious swing of his paw. Then, he wormed his way inside and looked up. A bunch of soot came drifting down onto his face and he had to shake his head to try and keep it from getting in his eyes.

Could he climb up there? The sky looked very

far away. The dog stood up on his hind legs, and stretched his front legs up as far as they would go. Then he tried to scrabble up the chimney walls, digging his claws into the spaces between the bricks. He made it up about four feet, before he lost his balance and fell. So he tried again, but only made it three feet this time. Why couldn't he be a better jumper? Mr. Callahan *needed* him. The dog kept trying, but he also kept falling. Finally, he lay on his side in the fireplace, covered with soot, with his claws throbbing. Three of them had actually gotten torn from his desperate attempt to climb up the narrow tunnel of bricks.

The dark room below the house. That's where he needed to go. The dog ran into the pantry and flung his body against the door to the basement. The latch didn't fasten very well, and his weight was enough to force the door open. Now he could go find help!

First, he returned to the living room to see if maybe Mr. Callahan was okay now. But he was still lying limply on the rug, with the cats huddled up next to him. Gently using his teeth, the dog pulled one of Mr. Callahan's slippers off. He carried it back to the cellar door and ran down the rickety steps.

The cellar was a dank, little room with nothing more than a furnace, a water heater, a workbench, and some wooden shelves where the

Callahans stored some of their tools and old magazines. The dog jumped on top of the workbench, and looked up at the small window above him. Could he jump that high? No. He tried a few times, but he didn't even come close.

He thought about Abigail, and some of her bad tricks, and he ran over to the bookcase. He climbed directly up the front of the shelves, as though it was a ladder, scrambling furiously until he was up on the very top of the bookcase. From there, it was easy to run along that shelf and jump over to the next one, which was right below a small window.

The only thing holding the window closed was a small hook. Lunging forward with both front paws stuck out in front of him, he was able to push the window free. It was short and narrow, but with a determined effort, he managed to worm through the opening and outside.

He had gotten out of the house! He could find help now!

The dog let the slipper fall from his mouth so that he could bark. Maybe someone would hear him, and come running. But no one came. He would have to go get someone, and bring them back here.

He picked up the slipper and then jumped over the gate. He could go to the place where his friend Dr. Kasanofsky worked, or to the place where he always found the nice men and women in the uniforms, or — the place where all of the teenagers in town went every day! *That's* where Gregory and Patricia were!

The dog ran down the street, keeping a steady, relentless pace. Some of the passing cars beeped their horns at him, but he didn't miss a step, or even look over, as he ran towards the high school.

Two senior boys who were skipping class and hanging out by the soccer field watched the blur of brown fur and churning legs tear past them, heading directly for the main entrance.

"Check it out, man," one of them drawled. "It's a bird. . . ."

"It's a plane," the other one said.

"It's Santa Paws!" they shouted at the same time, and then laughed and gave each other high-fives.

The dog hurled himself at the front doors, but they didn't open. So he dropped Mr. Callahan's slipper and started barking. He knew that if he barked long enough, someone would come to see what was wrong.

After a while, Ms. Oberlin, one of the office secretaries, peered outside. The soot-covered frantic animal banging his body against the doors was an alarming sight, until she realized that it was Santa Paws. She couldn't remember his ever coming to the high school during the middle of the day, and she was curious enough to go open the door for him.

"Hi, Santa Paws," Ms. Oberlin said. "What are you doing here?"

The dog snatched Mr. Callahan's slipper up from the ground and bolted right past her. Then he stopped in the main lobby, holding his paw up, and sniffing. Sometimes, he would ride in the car to this place, and watch sadly as Gregory and Patricia went inside with their backpacks, but he had never been in the building himself.

There were so many different scents, of so many different people and things, that it was almost impossible to distinguish them. But he sniffed, and sniffed, trying to locate one of the three scents he needed to find.

Hearing all of the noise, the principal, Mr. Gomez, came out of his office.

"Why is there a black wolf in the lobby?" he asked. "Is this another one of those infernal senior pranks?"

"No, sir," Ms. Oberlin said. "That's Santa Paws."

"Well," Mr. Gomez said mildly, "except for service animals, we really can't allow any pets to be on school property. Not even Santa Paws. Will you please show him out?"

"He seems — determined," Ms. Oberlin said.

"I thought that was the way he always was."

118

Mr. Gomez turned towards the main office. "Where is Mrs. Callahan assigned this period? I know it's her last day and all, but I really think she's going to need to come out and handle this."

Just then, the dog finally caught a whiff of someone dear and familiar. Patricia! And she was someplace close by! He tore down the hallway, concentrating intently on following the scent.

"Hey there, mister!" a teacher on hall monitor duty said as he raced by. "No running in the halls!"

The dog galloped straight towards the room where he knew Patricia was and burst through the swinging doors. It was the school library and one of the librarians automatically said, "*Shhh,*" in his direction. The dog looked around wildly. Where was she? He had to find her!

Patricia, who had a free study period, was lounging at a back table with Rachel and Spike, and Alex, the boy she sometimes dated. They had broken up at the Sadie Hawkins Dance in October, gotten back together again at the Thanksgiving Jamboree, but had decided to be "just friends" since the Winter Semi-Formal Dance.

"Well, that's weird," she said. "What's he doing here?" She let out a small whistle, and Santa Paws rushed over, dropping a grimy object in her lap.

"*Shhh!*" the librarian at the front desk said.

"Is that Santa Paws?" Rachel asked, turning her head to the side to listen. "It sounds like Santa Paws panting."

"Yeah," Patricia said. "He seems really upset. I'm not sure why he — " She looked down at her lap and suddenly recognized one of her father's Fred Flintstone slippers. At first, it didn't make any sense that Santa Paws would come all the way over here to give her a lost slipper, but then she understood what he was trying to tell her. "Oh, no."

"What?" Alex asked, worried by the look on her face. "Are you okay?"

"It's my father. Something must have happened to my father." She jumped up, clutching the slipper in one hand. "Sorry, I have to go."

She ran out of the library, with Santa Paws close behind her. She went straight to her mother's classroom and banged on the door, even though she was right in the middle of teaching a senior honors class.

Mrs. Callahan really hated being interrupted when she was trying to teach, and even though they spent every weekday in the same building, Patricia usually went out of her way to avoid bumping into her, because of what she usually described as a "multi-faceted conflict of interest."

"Excuse me," she said to her students, and stepped out into the hallway. "Can't this wait, Patricia? I'm in the middle of — "

"Santa Paws just brought me this," Patricia said, and showed her the slipper.

Mrs. Callahan's face paled, as she realized what that meant. But when she spoke, her voice was crisp and efficient.

"Go get Greg, and meet me in front of the school," she ordered. "He's in his geometry class." She saw a teacher's aide down the hall and snapped her fingers to get his attention. "Harvey! Come here, please. I need you to take over my class."

Without waiting to see if either of them was following her directions, she walked swiftly towards the teachers' room. She grabbed her coat and her briefcase, and hurried out to the teachers' parking lot. As she walked, she dialed home on her cell phone, to see if Mr. Callahan would answer the phone. This might be a false alarm — but if it was, it would be the first time Santa Paws had *ever* made a mistake like that in his life.

The phone rang and rang, until the answering machine picked up. She left a message, hoping that he was just busy working and would answer when he heard her voice — but, he didn't. She thought for a second, then dialed the police station to tell Uncle Steve what was going on, and to ask him to send a unit to the house right away.

Gregory and Patricia met her at the door, both

breathing hard and looking scared, with Santa Paws pacing back and forth behind them.

"Come on," she said, motioning them towards the car. "Steve's sending some officers over, so let's get home as fast as we can to let them in."

They all jumped into the car and Mrs. Callahan sped towards their house, with her hands clenched tightly around the steering wheel.

"Um, Mom?" Gregory ventured from the backseat. "Um, what if he's not home? I mean, with a slipper, he could still be — " anywhere — "out somewhere."

Mrs. Callahan's shoulders stiffened, since that was a definite possibility, but then she shook her head. "We'll start at the house. If he's not there, Santa Paws will be able to take us to him."

Gregory nodded, and none of them spoke for the rest of the ride.

Once they pulled into the driveway, Mrs. Callahan jumped out of the car with the motor still running. In fact, she was so worried that she actually left it in "Drive." Patricia lunged over from the passenger's side, put on the brake, shifted into "Park," and yanked the keys out of the ignition.

"Dad's okay, right?" Gregory asked. "I mean, he *has* to be."

Patricia couldn't think of an answer, but of course, she felt exactly the same way. "Just come on," she said.

They found their mother pounding on the backdoor, because she didn't have her keys. Patricia quickly pushed the house key into the lock, and her mother turned the knob and dashed into the house.

Santa Paws raced ahead of her, heading directly towards the den. They all ran after him, and when they got to the door, they stopped in horror.

Mr. Callahan was lying motionless on the floor!

11

All of the color rushed out of Mrs. Callahan's face as she saw her husband's still body — and two frightened cats crouching against him.

"911!" she said to Gregory. "*Now.*" Then she rushed forward and crouched down, putting her hand on his chest. When she felt his heart beating strongly, some of her initial terror faded. "All right. Okay. All right."

Both doorbells started ringing, and they could hear a voice yelling, "This is the police!"

"Go let them in, Patricia," Mrs. Callahan said, with her voice trembling.

Patricia obeyed without question, but Uncle Steve and two other officers were already inside the kitchen and getting ready to search the house.

"We're back here, Uncle Steve!" Patricia called. "Dad's in the den. We don't know what's wrong with him!"

The next half hour or so was a blur of activity.

Mr. Callahan's eyes had fluttered open at one point, and he mumbled, "It hurts," before fainting again. Even the paramedics weren't quite sure what was wrong with him, and so they did nothing more than take his vital signs and get an IV going before bundling him out to the waiting ambulance.

Gregory and Patricia stood in the driveway uncertainly as their mother jumped into the back of the ambulance and it sped away with its sirens wailing.

"It's all right, kids," Uncle Steve said. He was terribly worried about his big brother, but he didn't want upset his niece and nephew any more than they already were. "Let's make sure the animals are okay, lock up the house, and head over to the Emergency Room."

Gregory and Patricia did exactly what they were told, each pausing only long enough to give Santa Paws and the cats big hugs before they left.

At the hospital, they spent a very long time in the waiting room before their family doctor, Dr. Jennings, came out to talk to them. Her face was somewhat strained, but she was also smiling a little, so they assumed that the news must not be as terrible as they had feared.

"He's finishing up in surgery," Dr. Jennings said. "His appendix was just beginning to rupture when they brought him in. He'll be spending about a week here, while we monitor him for infection, but barring any complications — which I don't foresee at the moment — he should be back to his normal self in no time."

Mrs. Callahan let out her breath, and sat down so quickly that it seemed as though she might be afraid her legs were going to give out. "Thank you, Rebecca," she said.

"I'm just happy to be able to give you good news," Dr. Jennings said. "Had he been complaining of any pain lately?"

Gregory thought back, guiltily, to sitting at the breakfast table that morning. "He said he had a stomachache, but that he was fine."

Dr. Jennings grinned wryly. "So much for his abilities as a diagnostician, then. He may want to stick to writing books." She paused. "My understanding is that Santa Paws came to the school to alert you?"

They all nodded.

"A few extra Milk-Bones tonight, then, hmm?" Dr. Jennings said, and turned to go. "I'll let you know when they take him down to Recovery. You should be able to see him shortly after that."

After Dr. Jennings left, Mrs. Callahan rested her head in her hands.

"Are you okay, Mom?" Patricia asked. "Do you want anything?"

"I want to give that dog a thousand *cases* of

Milk-Bones," Mrs. Callahan said, and then put her head back in her hands.

It was a long day. Uncle Steve and Aunt Emily came to stay in the waiting room with them, and Gregory and Patricia's grandparents were driving down from Vermont. They had been planning to spend Christmas — and Miranda's birthday — in Oceanport, anyway, but now they were going to arrive a day early.

At first, only Mrs. Callahan was allowed to go in and visit, but finally, Gregory and Patricia were permitted to see their father, too. He was lying in a hospital bed, looking tired, and pale, and as though he needed a shave.

He smiled at them weakly. "I guess it was finally my turn to be saved by Santa Paws."

"Looks that way, yeah," Gregory said, his smile just as weak.

Mrs. Callahan was going to spend the night at the hospital, so Aunt Emily drove Gregory and Patricia home when visiting hours ended.

"Do you two need anything, or are you okay?" she asked. "Your grandparents should get here in another hour or two."

"We're fine," Patricia said. "Thanks for bringing us home, though."

But once they got in the house, they were both so tired that they sat at the kitchen table without moving. The combination of being at the hospital, and worrying so much about their father, had been absolutely exhausting. Three anxious — and *hungry* — pets ran out to greet them, and Patricia managed to muster up enough energy to feed them, while Gregory refilled their water dish.

"You think either of us is going to be able to stay awake until Grammy and Granddad get here?" she asked.

Gregory shook his head, already barely able to keep his eyes open. "Not a chance," he said.

And, he turned out to be right.

The Callahans spent Christmas Eve at the hospital. Mr. Callahan was feeling somewhat stronger, but he was only allowed to sip water and broth, and when they turned on the television, he fell asleep before the first commercial.

"He *is* okay," Gregory whispered to his mother, "right?"

Mrs. Callahan nodded. "He's fine. Abdominal surgery is tough, that's all." She had had a C-section when she gave birth to Gregory, and she remembered how difficult the recovery had been. She glanced at Gregory and Patricia, who were both slouching in uncomfortable chairs. "Do you two want to go home for a while? You look so tired."

They *were* tired, but they shook their heads firmly. It was Christmas Eve, and they wanted

128

to keep their parents company as long as possible.

"All right, you can stay for another couple of hours," Mrs. Callahan said. "But after Grammy and Granddad take you to Miranda's party, I think you should go home and get some sleep."

"It's Christmas Eve," Gregory pointed out. "Can't we please come back, and spend it with you and Dad?"

Mrs. Callahan wanted to say no, but she didn't like the idea of the family being separated tonight, either.

"Okay," she said reluctantly. "But if either of you get too exhausted, you have to *promise* that you'll tell me, so I can have someone drive you back to the house."

Gregory and Patricia nodded, although they had no intention of doing any such thing. What they really wished was that their father would be able to come home with them tonight, but they knew that that wasn't going to be possible so soon after his operation.

They sat and watched television with their mother, while Mr. Callahan slept, although none of them were really paying attention to anything that was happening on the screen.

"Did you ever notice that we always seem to spend Christmas Eve in a hospital room?" Patricia asked.

Four years earlier, she and Gregory had been

in a hospital in New Hampshire, after recovering from a plane crash. Santa Paws had been forced to lead them miles through the snowy mountains to save them. Then, two years ago, Mrs. Callahan had been the one in the hospital, after she broke her leg badly when her car crashed during a violent ice storm. Naturally, Santa Paws had been the one to rescue her. And only last year, they had been at Mass General Hospital in Boston, after Gregory got hypothermia while trying to help Santa Paws recover a boy who had fallen through the ice at the Swan Pond.

"Maybe next year, we should all spend the entire week before Christmas staying in the house, hiding under the covers," Mrs. Callahan said.

It was a funny image, but Gregory and Patricia couldn't help thinking that it might be a pretty smart idea, too.

Back at home, the dog was lonely and nervous and unhappy. He paced around the house for hours, moving from room to room, over and over again. The cats had lost patience with him, and Evelyn retreated to the linen closet, while Abigail squirmed inside a partially-packed box of dishes. The dog wished that he could find a place to relax, too, but instead, he paced and wandered and roamed.

At one point, Grammy stopped by to take him for a walk. The dog was glad to be able to stretch his legs, but he wanted to get home as soon as possible, because he didn't want to miss seeing the Callahans the second they came back from wherever they had gone.

Grammy fed all three pets, patted them, changed the litter box, and then went over to Uncle Steve and Aunt Emily's house. Even with the turmoil at the hospital, and the fact that it was Christmas Eve, no one in the family wanted to forget that it was also Miranda's birthday today. Mr. Callahan might not be able to come to the party, but everyone else in the family needed to be there to participate in the celebration, at least for a little while.

Alone again, the dog resumed his pacing. Had something very, very bad happened to Mr. Callahan? Was that why his family wasn't here? He rested his paws on a windowsill in the living room, gazing outside and wishing that he would see the family station wagon rumbling up the street. But all he could see was the yard, the big trees with their bare, empty branches, and a few snowflakes starting to fall on the sodden ground.

Finally, he couldn't stand it anymore. He ran down to the basement, climbed up the bookcase, and squeezed out through the skinny window.

He was going to go find his family!

Gregory and Patricia and Mrs. Callahan didn't go home until almost ten o'clock that night. Mr.

Callahan could still only sip water or clear broth, but they had wanted to stay and keep him company during dinner, anyway. And once visiting hours started, an endless stream of concerned Oceanport citizens trooped in and out of his room, with flowers, and candy, and other thoughtful gifts.

Most of them understood that Mr. Callahan was too tired to talk for very long and would leave after five or ten minutes. But a few well-meaning people plopped themselves down in the chairs next to his bed to gab away as long as possible.

Mr. Callahan sighed as one particularly long-winded, if pleasant, older lady finally left the room.

"I know they're just trying to be nice," he said hoarsely. "But — well — "

Mrs. Callahan stood up, with a determined tilt to her chin. "I'll be right back."

She went directly to the nurses' station and asked if there was any way that Mr. Callahan's visits could be suspended for the rest of the night. The nurses were happy to do that, and one of them, who took art lessons at the Oceanport Gallery every other Friday, sat down and drew an intricate "No Visitors, Please" sign with red Magic Marker. Then she taped it on Mr. Callahan's door, and the family had a chance to be alone together.

The only exceptions to the rule were Grammy, Granddad, Uncle Steve, and Aunt Emily — and when they saw how tired Mr. Callahan was, even they only stayed for about fifteen minutes each. Down in New York, Aunt Laurel and Pedro and Kate had been very worried, too, but Mr. Callahan managed to talk to each of them on the phone briefly, which made them feel better.

"I'm sorry. It's not much of a Christmas, with me stuck in here," Mr. Callahan said softly, when the family was alone together.

"All that matters is that you're okay now, Dad," Patricia said. "That makes it a *great* Christmas."

Gregory nodded. "A *totally* great Christmas."

As they got ready to go, Mr. Callahan had fallen asleep again before they even got to the door.

"He'll feel better tomorrow, right?" Gregory asked.

"Of course he will," Mrs. Callahan assured him. "Come on, let's go home and see those poor pets of ours."

When they drove up their street, they could see that their house was completely dark.

Mrs. Callahan shook her head in dismay. "We really should have left some lights on in there. That looks so depressing."

They went inside and began turning on all of the lights, including the Christmas tree. Abigail and Evelyn came running downstairs, eager to be patted and cuddled. But there was one thing missing.

Santa Paws!

The dog had been running through Oceanport for the last few hours, looking for the Callahans. He went to the school, he went to the Catholic Church, he went to the beach, and he went to the park. After that, he ran to the mall, and the grocery store, and the post office, and up and down Main Street until he had checked all of the small stores and restaurants.

But the Callahans were nowhere to be seen.

The dog decided to start at one end of town, and check every single street, one at a time. He ran past the Jorgensens' farm, past the Little League baseball field, past the tennis courts, and past the elementary school.

Where could they be?

But then, he stopped when a surprising thought came into his mind.

He had been out and about in Oceanport for several hours, and *no one* had needed to be rescued. He didn't think that had ever happened before. Was he so worried about the Callahans that he wasn't paying attention to the problems other people might be having? He sat back on his haunches to sniff the air and try to decide whether he had overlooked anything.

For the first time he could ever remember, the entire town felt safe. It was Christmas Eve, people were sound asleep in their beds, and every single one of them was safe. No one needed rescuing, no one needed help.

No one needed *him*.

The dog looked around and saw that he was on the old Kenyon bridge. It had been built during the 1930s, and it stood above a wide river which ran straight to the sea. He lifted his front paws up onto the cement railing, closed his eyes, and inhaled deeply. It was very strange, but he couldn't smell *anything*, other than the fresh ocean air.

It smelled nice, but it made him a little bit sad to think that there was no one in Oceanport who needed his help right now. Feeling very lonely, the dog lowered his head and walked across the bridge with his tail dragging on the ground.

He would just have to go home, by himself, and hope that his family would come home soon. He missed them *so much*.

Then, out of nowhere, he felt that mysterious, powerful feeling return deep inside his chest. It felt warm, and strong, and secure. He stopped walking, because suddenly, everything around him looked very bright. It was almost as though the sun was coming up early, or a star was falling out of the sky.

The dog stopped and raised one paw in the air.

It didn't make sense, but the light *was* coming from the sky. It rushed towards him, moving faster and faster, and casting a white glow over the entire bridge. Then, just as he was afraid that the ray of light might crash right through him, it shot past him, over the bridge, and straight into the water with a massive splash.

Then, it was dark again. In fact, he had never seen anything so dark.

He whined uneasily, not sure if he should run away, or try to figure out what had just happened. He was about to start running when his whole body began to tingle. He stopped again, shivering from the intensity of the feeling. What was happening? Why did he feel this way?

Then he heard it. It was a small sad sound, barely loud enough to be noticed over the wind and the water. But, he heard it. Was it a squeak? Or a squeal? Or a desperate cry from someone who felt even more alone than he did?

Someone, or some*thing*, needed his help, after all!

12

The sound seemed to be coming directly from the churning water and the dog ran back to the middle of the bridge to try and get a closer look. He stared intently down at the rushing current. Then he saw a small head bobbing up and down in the water.

Without a second thought, he soared off the bridge, high in the air, and into the freezing water. It was so cold that it seemed to penetrate all the way through him, but he was too busy to care. He swam directly towards the little head, which seemed to be whimpering now. He realized, as he got closer, that it was a puppy!

It didn't make sense that a puppy would be floating in the water, out in the middle of nowhere, but the dog didn't worry about that. He grabbed the puppy gently by the nape of the neck, and towed it over to the riverbank. He deposited the puppy onto the marshy ground and then climbed out of the water himself.

They both shook vigorously to get rid of as much water as possible, and then sat down to look at each other.

The puppy was about four months old, with soft, black fur. Her eyes seemed unusually bright and clear, and she looked at him with total adoration. For a split second, he thought that the powerful shining light from the sky was now beaming down directly on them, but he knew that that was impossible. So he blinked a few times, until the light went away.

The dog could see that she wasn't wearing a collar, and this wasn't a puppy he had ever noticed living in Oceanport before. Her silky fur was wet and tangled, and she was thin and neglected. But he could tell from the warm feeling in his heart that this was a very special little dog, and that he wanted her to come home with him and live with the Callahans forever.

The puppy's little legs were still wobbly, so he carried her up the embankment to the street. Then he set her on her feet. She wagged her tiny tail at him, and he wagged his tail back at her. What a nice puppy! He loved this puppy!

She was too tired to walk yet, so he carried her down the street. His house was several miles away, and it was going to take a long time to get there.

This part of Oceanport had very few houses,

and they were surrounded by woods on both sides of the street. As the dog walked steadily along, he had an eerie sense that he was being watched. He looked at the woods, and saw small glowing lights everywhere. They were yellow, and green, and orange — and he realized that they were eyes, staring at him!

He stopped in horror, and let the puppy slip down to the ground. What were all of those eyes? Why were they looking at them so intently?

The eyes moved closer, and gradually, he saw that they belonged to various wild animals. There were squirrels and skunks and field mice and opossums and raccoons and deer and chipmunks and even a muskrat or two. The animals kept coming forward until they had formed a small circle around Santa Paws and the puppy.

There was a large fluttering sound, and the dog looked up to see hundreds of birds flying down to join the circle. He knew he should be afraid, but for some reason, he wasn't anymore. The circle of wildlife felt protective. It felt *safe*.

After a few minutes, the birds and wild animals withdrew without ever having uttered a single sound, and he and the puppy were left alone on the street again. He looked down at her, very confused, and she just wagged her tail calmly. He started to pick her up, but she struggled until he put her down again. Then, she trotted along next to him, trying to make her skinny little legs move exactly the way his did.

It was dawn now, on Christmas Day. All over Oceanport, people were waking up to get ready to go to church, or eat breakfast, or do whatever their family enjoyed doing on the holiday.

As they traveled across town, the dog noticed that lots of pets were looking out the windows of their houses at them. Whenever they passed a dog who happened to be outside in its backyard, it would stop what it was doing, let out a single respectful bark, and then stand still until they had passed.

It felt incredible to see all of those dogs and cats and parakeets and guinea pigs and other pets staring out their windows in house, after house, after house. The dog couldn't quite make sense of the situation, but he knew that the animals were watching them with affection, and maybe even pride. This made the dog feel very happy and he wagged his tail constantly as he and the puppy moved through the streets.

He didn't know exactly what was happening today, but so far, he really liked it!

After they got home the night before, Gregory and Patricia had gone outside to call Santa Paws repeatedly, until their mother finally made them go to bed. They had hoped that he would be waiting for them at the backdoor when they woke up, but unfortunately, he wasn't there.

"He does this *every* Christmas," Mrs. Callahan reminded them. "Please don't worry. He's probably just out there rescuing people."

"But there haven't been any news reports," Gregory said. He and Patricia had both tuned their clock radios to the local public access station and let them play all night long. They had been hoping that if someone broke in with a special report about their dog, they would wake up when they heard his name and know that he was safe.

Mrs. Callahan was worried, too, but she was trying not to show it. "It's Christmas, Greg. There probably aren't more than a couple of reporters even working today."

Gregory and Patricia weren't convinced that was true — Christmas was always a *very* active news day in Oceanport — but they nodded, because they knew it would make their mother feel better.

They waited, and waited, until it was almost time for visiting hours at the hospital to start.

"Do you two want to stay here, and come over later?" Mrs. Callahan asked. "I know your father will understand."

Gregory and Patricia were torn, but they decided to accompany her to the hospital, since it was Christmas morning, and their father must

141

be feeling very lonely. It was important to find Santa Paws, but it was important to go see their father, too.

They carried a stack of presents out to the car to bring to the hospital. Mrs. Callahan had hung some ribbons and Christmas lights in Mr. Callahan's room the day before, to try and make the atmosphere seem more festive. She had even gotten a wreath and put it in his hospital window.

Since Abigail was a certified Pet Therapy cat, she was coming along today, and Mrs. Callahan had gotten special permission to bring Evelyn, too, as long as she stayed in Mr. Callahan's room and didn't wander around the halls. The doctors and nurses wanted to do anything possible to make their patients feel happy, since the holidays were such a difficult time to be in the hospital.

"Your uncle says the whole department is on alert, and they'll be making regular patrols past the house," Mrs. Callahan said, as they drove towards Oceanport Memorial. "If anyone finds him, they'll bring him straight over to the hospital to see us."

Gregory and Patricia nodded, and did their best to smile.

Christmas just wasn't going to feel like Christmas without Santa Paws.

The dog and the puppy kept trotting towards the Callahans' house, their progress slow but steady as the dog adjusted his gait to fit the puppy's smaller strides. He had expected her to get tired and need to rest, but so far, she seemed to be unusually plucky.

He was about to turn down their street, when he sensed that that wasn't the right place to go this time. The Callahans were someplace else, he could *feel* it. But he was pretty sure he had checked the entire town, without finding them. He looked down at the puppy, who wagged her tail encouragingly.

Then, it came to him. Mr. Callahan had been lying down. He had to be very, very sick. That meant that he must be in the big building where the dog always went to visit the people lying in beds!

Abruptly, the dog spun around and headed towards the hospital. The puppy joined him without missing a beat, and they trotted faster than before, running through the quiet, peaceful streets. When the dog finally saw the hospital up ahead of him, he barked happily because the Callahans' station wagon was parked right out front! His family was here!

He brought the puppy up to the main door, which opened automatically. The puppy hung back, because she had never been inside a big, noisy building like this. Actually, the dog didn't know it, but the puppy had never been inside *any* kind of building before.

So, the dog deftly scooped her up and carried her down the hall.

A passing orderly recognized him.

"Hey, Santa Paws," he said. "Merry Christmas."

The dog wagged his tail in response, but he didn't pause.

Right now, he just wanted to find his family!

Mr. Callahan had woken up feeling much better, and the nurses let them move down to the sunroom to open their Christmas presents. Grammy and Granddad, and Uncle Steve and Aunt Emily, and Miranda and Lucy were all there, too. Mr. Callahan had realized right away that there was someone very important missing, but after a quick glance at his wife, he didn't mention it, and they all pretended to be having a wonderful time. They called New York, and all took turns talking on the phone, wishing Aunt Laurel and Pedro and Kate a Merry Christmas. When Kate asked happily what Santa Paws and the cats had gotten for Christmas, Mrs. Callahan just said, smoothly, "Oh, treats and toys and all sorts of wonderful things. Now, tell me about *your* gifts."

Out in the hallway, Gregory could hear people saying, "Hi!" and "Merry Christmas!" in happy voices. He didn't really pay attention until he heard someone say, "Happy holidays, Santa

Paws!" He jumped up and stood in the doorway to see if it might be true.

Down at the end of the hall, Santa Paws was running directly towards him, carrying something in his mouth.

"Hey, he's here!" Gregory shouted to the rest of the family. "He's okay!"

The dog ran into the room and greeted everyone joyfully. Here was his family! All together! What a wonderful day! He was especially happy to see Mr. Callahan sitting up and looking just like himself. In fact, he was so happy that he had to bark a few times, even though he was supposed to be quiet when he was visiting the hospital.

In all of the excitement, it took a few minutes before anyone noticed that he hadn't come to the hospital alone. There was a small black puppy, sitting shyly by the door.

Abigail promptly took it upon herself to investigate this intruder up close. She glared at the puppy through narrowed eyes, and then hauled her paw back to smack her. But the puppy just stared evenly at her, and after a second or two, Abigail lowered her paw.

Evelyn also walked over to examine the puppy suspiciously, hissing the entire time. For some reason, though, the puppy wasn't frightened at all. So, Abigail and Evelyn jumped onto a nearby table, where they could watch her disapprovingly, but also take some time out to wash their faces.

"Whose puppy is that?" Miranda asked. "Is it for me?"

"P'ppy!" Lucy yelled.

"Well, I don't know," Mrs. Callahan said, and glanced over at Uncle Steve and Aunt Emily. "The puppy might already have an owner, Miranda, or — "

Patricia shook her head. "I don't think so, Mom. Look how thin she is. And her coat is all scraggly, too."

Santa Paws pranced over to the door, and then brought the puppy around to meet each member of the family in turn. They all took turns patting her, and admiring her, and the dog was very pleased that she got such a friendly reception. Abigail and Evelyn even relented enough to come down from the table.

Although they knew that their grandparents, or their aunt and uncle, would be happy to adopt a new pet, Gregory and Patricia looked at their parents, hoping that they were going to be able to keep the puppy themselves. She was happy and lively — and had somehow managed to make friends with the cats in under a minute.

"I know, I know," Mrs. Callahan said, able to guess what they were thinking. "But we already have three pets, and since we're about to pack up and move, I'm not sure if this is a good time to — " She stopped in mid-sentence, as she saw Santa Paws place the puppy on a small rug and then lie down next to her, wagging his tail non-stop. He looked very content. In fact, his expression was almost *blissful*.

"Maybe it doesn't matter if we want a new puppy," Gregory said slowly. "Maybe it doesn't matter if it's the right time, or convenient, or anything like that. I mean, he never asks for anything, and maybe this time, all that matters is what *Santa Paws* wants."

They all looked over at Santa Paws again. He was wagging his tail, and resting a protective paw across the puppy as she yawned and closed her eyes for a long-overdue nap. Abigail and Evelyn were somewhat disgruntled by this turn of events, but they went over and curled up on the rug, too.

"I think Santa Paws wants a puppy," Miranda said, suddenly sounding much older than her age.

It was so obviously true that no one could disagree with her.

Mr. Callahan let out his breath. "Well, okay, then. I guess we have a new puppy. Merry Christmas, Santa Paws!"

"You'd better call Kate back, and let her know what he actually *did* get for Christmas," Patricia said to her mother.

Mrs. Callahan grinned wryly. "I think maybe I'd better warn *Aunt Laurel* about what he got

147

for Christmas," she said, and reached for the telephone again. Luckily, Aunt Laurel was very fond of animals, too, and had a cranky grey and white cat of her own. She was probably going to be surprised to hear the news, but she would definitely be enthusiastic about it.

From the way Gregory and Patricia came over and started playing with the puppy, the dog knew at once that she was now the newest member of the family. He barked and wagged his tail, and the puppy joined in, which made everyone else in the room laugh, and say, "Merry Christmas, Santa Paws!"

The dog couldn't remember ever feeling so happy. He was here, with his family, and now, he had a new friend, too.

This was going to be the most wonderful Christmas ever!

Don't wait for Christmas!
Enjoy SANTA PAWS all year round.

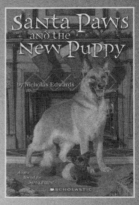